C0-FQH-725

LIVES OF MAPMAKERS

Lives of Mapmakers

Alicia L. Conroy

Carnegie Mellon University Press
2006

Several of these stories have been published, sometimes in slightly different forms: "The Nameless Season" in *Rosebud*, "Mud-Colored Beauties of the Plains" in *Ploughshares*, "Bad Hand" in *Ontario Review*, "Women Who Dream of Corn" in *Chattahoochee Review*, "The One Thing I'm Good At" in *Puerto del Sol*, "What the Body Learns" in *New Delta Review*, and a version of "All This Talking About God" in the prize volume *O. Henry Festival Stories 2000.*

Book Design: Tara Sakauye
Cover Design: Leif Kolt

Library of Congress Control Number: 2005933842
ISBN-13: 978-0-88748-451-3
ISBN-10: 0-88748-451-4
Copyright © 2006 by Alicia L. Conroy
All rights reserved
Printed and bound in the United States of America

10 9 8 7 6 5 4 3 2 1

Acknowledgements

I have many people to thank for their encouragement and assistance, first among them my family: Mom, Ethan, Peter, Penny, Ann & Bob, Carrie, and Cynthia; my friends in Boston, New York and Minneapolis; and Christopher Schmid, who gave me a room for writing and so much more.

My amazing teachers have included Carmi Soifer, June Spence, and my thesis advisors: Wendell Mayo at Bowling Green State Univ. and Ann Doyle at Mount Holyoke College. Special thanks to Karen Craigo and Mike Czyzniejewski for their friendship and critiques, and super-special thanks to Bonnie Jo Campbell, Melissa Fraterrigo, Donna Sparkman, Rachael Perry—wonderful writers, critics, and friends, and each one an inspiration to me.

I'm grateful to Laura Williams for her advice and assistance, and to Sharon Dilworth at Carnegie Mellon University Press for believing in this collection. I need to thank Keith Banner and Dustin Parsons for their help with "Bad Hand," Don Lee for his suggestions on "Mud-Colored Beauties of the Plains," and *Eclectic Literary Forum* for my first publication and my first award.

One section in the title story was inspired by Douglas McNaughton's 2000 article in *Mercator's World* magazine and the responses to it. The Devines and Charles Denny and family endowed college and university awards that have helped me stay the course.

In memory of my father, Lawrence E. Conroy,
and the others who have gone on ahead.

Contents

MUD-COLORED BEAUTIES OF THE PLAINS

Mucking around in the slimy, extinct creek-bed was dirty heaven for most of the second-grade boys and girls, who immediately armed themselves with gooey objects to slide down necks of each other's T-shirts—all except fastidious little Lily Fusco. Of course, this is why she discovered the body.

The girl had moved away from her mud-loving classmates to search the banks in peace, and something smooth and shiny caught her eye. She was doing as she'd been told; she filled a blue bucket with some murky water from a sinkhole and plodded across pudding-thick mud in her rain-boots. In a long, slow curve of the once-filled streambed she poured, to clear the silt from what was surely a treasure lodged against a tree-root: old clam shell, a rock teeming with trilobites.

Years before, Mrs. Sundquist's classes had gone there to find live things. Today the creek was almost completely dry; the housing development upstream had seen to that over a decade ago. At best, the bed was ten feet across, but those as old as Mrs. Sundquist, over thirty, recalled the flow: barely knee-deep, just enough current to brighten the stony shingle below, which had hidden salamanders under flat slabs of limestone, formed a nursery for little crayfish. Now, the bed held only run-off; and lanky boxelder, alder, and cottonwood seedlings stretched from the mud. Her students these days went to glean fossils from stacked sedimentary ledges protruding from clay-rich soil in the banks, to pull artifacts of fluvial life from amid tree roots and marsh marigolds.

Lily, finding an object with promise, rubbed with the long-handled brush she'd been given. She scrubbed, gently; trickled water, scrubbed and trickled, and a furrowed shape began to emerge from the root, around the bright spot, mother-of-pearl. Lily shrieked with pitch so achingly high and true that even the boys stopped their gloppy horseplay and turned around.

The teacher, seeing it was Lily and that she was upright and perfectly intact, glanced over the students and took her time picking her slippery way over there.

Lily had dropped her pail and was broadcasting intermittent signals, high and clear like the shrieking whistle at the sheet-metal plant. Lily; Lily, intoned Mrs. Sundquist soothingly, edging her way across slick rock and mud. Calm down. Did those boys scare you?

But Lily wriggled no creepy-crawlies from her T-shirt; she stood still, pointing, stabbing a finger down at the creek bed. The teacher stooped, peered. It was a pale greenish fingernail.

Lily, come here, honey, said Mrs. Sundquist, very quietly. My, that root looks kind of like a finger, doesn't it? No wonder you were scared.

She couldn't resist giving the thing one more little swish with the girl's brush; a hand, all right. She bent towards the girl and put a finger to her lips. Let's not scare the others, shall we? she whispered, and the little girl nodded, lip trembling, her brown braids bobbing.

Mrs. Sundquist took her by the hand and called to the other second-graders scurrying about, and when they didn't come, said: Counting! One, two, three, four, . . . and boys and girls scrambled over the banks and crept from under trees and converged together. I think it's getting kind of hot today, she said cheerily, anybody for ice cream?

Whoops and chirps, clatter to collect buckets and rocks, a great rush toward the mini-bus, because usually when she counted it meant trouble, and never, never ice cream.

As she herded them toward the bus, the teacher cast a look back over her shoulder and fought a shudder.

The cops and the coroners spent a good deal of time taking pictures with measuring rulers before they disturbed the mud. They sluiced gently with water to take off the bulk of the clinging brown silt, the better to see the body's contours. They bent and cautiously removed most of the mud coating, in gloved handfuls. A mud-veiled face, a thin, flat-chested trunk, suggested a youth, male or female; but the legs wouldn't give up their silty coating, like a drape of blanket. The coroner tested the arm, scraping with his gloved finger, saw how well the flesh seemed to be preserved; it didn't pulp or shred. That mud made a tidy coating, he noted, clay sealing the skin from edema, from aerobic microbes. A muscousy mass around the nose and mouth. Carefully, they began to pry up the carcass, and during an up-thrust of the round-edged spade the body said, Ow.

The patrolman dropped the spade, letting the shoulder slip back down. Ow, whispered the brown lips again.

Jenkins, the coroner, gestured for more buckets of sludgy water, slopped little splashes on the sideways face, the brows, the brown-clad lips—a moan. Just gas escaping, he said. Then two, three bucketfuls dashed over the body. The shape very slowly slid toward one side, almost appeared to tremble. Curiosity got the better of Jenkins, and he lowered his portly pale form, put his clean ear to the dark, slippery chest and felt the tremor, heard the impossibly slow, impossibly real syncopation within. And yet there was no breath hissing from the lips, no rise and fall of the sternum.

Groenig, take a listen, he ordered, kneeling back; I'm hearing things. His younger assistant gingerly knelt in the mud, wiped feebly at the skin, pressed his face alongside; his eyes widened and brightened, his face turned the question to his boss.

I'll be damned, said Jenkins. Now this is ugly.

It was only after the ambulance arrived and the mud had been further wiped away that they discovered how something, apparently in odd, semi-anaerobic decay, had melted and fused over the legs so that the genitalia vanished and the limbs softened and merged, perhaps in rigor, like the tail of a large brown tadpole. Yet the EKG kept up a steady, strange rhythm—noting not the usual *lup-dub* but a slow *bump . . . bump . . .* , and long after they were sure the next *bump* wasn't coming at all, a galloping *kitty-kitty-kitty Bump.*

Persistent vegetative coma, the junior EMT said confidently, as he hooked up an I.V. in the arm.

I've heard of survival without oxygen in cold-water hypothermia, replied his female partner, but it's April, for Christ's sakes, and where's the water?

But when they swabbed the inert face with alcohol wipes, it remained brown and cold, the lips breathless under the oxygen mask.

Later at the hospital it was the ER nurse, gently wiping the muddy, degraded legs with a moist towel, who noticed the round, dull scales left behind on the terry cloth. After a hurried conference with the attending, the nurse manager, and an intern, they carted the mysterious carcass to the shower, lowered the gurney gently down, undid the EKG leads, and let lukewarm water play over the figure.

After only two or three minutes, first one creaseless eyelid then the other popped open, revealing orbs all hazel-green iris with no white. The lips shuddered apart, sipping then expelling air at last: ohhh.

Yup, said Doc Hastings, who was due to retire in a couple months; Well, I never. He rubbed at his wiry white hair. What we got here is some kinda hibernating mermaid, I expect.

It gazed at them, strange eyes appearing mildly astonished, head lolling like it was drunk or very sleepy.

Okay. Doc Hastings's large hand scraped back and forth across his mouth. Give her thirty minutes in here at 65 degrees. Then we'll see. And put some restraints on the thorax and tail so she don't roll off, he instructed.

Right, said the nurse, Atwood, staring at their patient.

Start a glucose drip—no wait, god knows what we got, let's run some chemistry first, Doc said. And for pity's sake, be careful on the draw. I'll tell the desk you're monitoring. You—he poked a finger at the intern—come with me. When the intern stalled, he barked, You can do your gawking later, hop to!

Atwood, the nurse who'd noticed the scales, sat with the creature as it slowly shook awake. First a flex and release of shoulders, a shudder in the tail, a slow undulation beginning at the little finger which had so shocked Lily. The creature began to pulse and stretch like a sleepy schoolgirl. The nurse turned off the shower, daubed at the clammy skin, draped the being carefully with a johnny to cover its body. The olive-drab creature blinked, then slowly clasped the edge of the fabric and pulled it away carefully, let it drop to the wet tile floor. She held still except for a tremor, watching Atwood with eyes that appeared wary.

The nurse summoned the doctor and the chastened intern, who moved slowly and whispered. It didn't look like what any of them would call a mermaid. All over, the creature was an olive-tan color, from hair to tail, slightly deeper at the tail-tip. It surely wasn't a picture-book mermaid—there was no brightly scaled trunk, no whale-like flipper, nothing voluptuously female and human. On this creature, the normal ellipse of a somewhat flat-breasted human torso tapered to a cylinder at the waist, then flattened into a muscular, eel-like end with continuous, rippling fins above and below. The spine dove centrally into the torso at the waist. Smalls scales glinted only faintly. Upon close inspection, there were a half-dozen pale aqua dots, each no bigger than a pencil eraser, running down the midline of the lower, scaled body—it was hard to say where "tail" began—on either side. A pale-green scar, an arc about twelve inches long, rose on the back below the dorsal fin and behind what would be the left knee. Sparse, fine hair clung over vestigial ears, merest flaps of flesh protecting the ear canals. Ribs, collarbones, and face-bones protruded clearly. A fine musculature, perhaps slightly wasted, showed through thin, fatless skin. No noteworthy breasts or external genitalia showed, but perhaps from a narrowness of shoulders, perhaps from the mythological precedent, they were inclined to call it a she.

How did you know? whispered Atwood.

Doc Hastings coughed, a-hep-hep-hep, in the way he did when talking to pesky medical students and administrators. Well, you know. Just something I heard about once or twice.

Man, the others won't believe this! said Furnari, the intern. Wait till they see it.

Doc's brows charged together. Don't you breathe a word of this till I talk to some people, neither of you! he growled. Let's just call this quarantine for the moment. I mean it, he said to Furnari, I'll can your little pipsqueak ass, so help me.

And he'll do it, too, said Atwood to the gaping intern, I've seen him.

You bet, Doc growled.

The creature—it, she—watched them with unblinking, weed-green eyes.

Doc Hastings's neighbor Chuck had an above-ground pool that he didn't use much now that his kids had all left home. They drained it, and the fire department sent a tanker to load up with water from the Green River, which didn't have as much heavy metal and dioxin contamination, and they used that to fill the pool. Doc swore them all to secrecy, partly by letting Chuck pretend to be FBI, which he did by hastily flashing his video rental card. The biology professor who'd come over from the university told Chuck he might get a little algae build-up, but to keep the water circulating and aerated. Chuck strung his laundry line a little higher on the other neighbors' side and hung his tarps and tents on it.

The humans all watched the mermaid slip into the pool with a squirm of urgency or relief. She plunged straight down and stayed there; after 86 seconds she somersaulted, circled down, breached the surface again, shook her lank hair, seemed to smile. The long, eel-like tail seemed less like a defect in the water; it flexed and rippled, undulated the flanged dorsal and ventral fins. For the first hour she patiently circled the pool walls, its bottom. Then she swam submerged to the eyes, watching them. How fascinating, the biology professor kept saying. He couldn't believe his own eyes. Fascinating. Mud-puppy, moray. Tadpole.

Tadpole? What does it turn into? said a second professor, an anthropologist.

Oh, it just looks like a tadpole, said the first. I think.

Doc Hastings said, It just hibernates through the winters. Tucks down into the silt and nods off.

The biologist gaped, then nodded. So, uh, I guess the current of the spring snowmelt brings them around again. He wondered out loud whether the mermaid had lain there with her reduced metabolism for perhaps twelve years, since drainage ditches of the housing development had starved the narrow creek, or even decades longer. He had never heard of a freshwater mermaid, a prairie mermaid, a mermaid hibernating under frost-rimed cottonwoods.

Oh, sure, said Doc Hastings, rubbing at the bristles in one ear. I mean, the stories go . . . . My grandpa used to say, but nobody took him seriously . . . . He said spirits in the cornfield, meteor craters past the fairgrounds, too. Those old-timers were full of great stories. Not so many old-timers left around here. Hem. Look how she's watching us. Wonder if there's others podded down in other cricks.

Or if she's the last one, the biologist said.

Indigenous, the second professor guessed. Lakota, Arikara, she said, looking at the mermaid's greeny-brown skin, but mostly at the planes of her face, the nose, the broad cheekbones, brow. She could be a missing link.

The face looks human, but it's those eyes that get you, said Doc. All green, no visible sclera, wide and fishy. To himself he thought, Something wise in there, and wild, too.

At first she gobbled as if she truly hadn't eaten in years. To ascertain her tastes, over the next days they gave her an array of edibles, human and aquatic, from ravioli to pemmican, maggots to crayfish, arrowroot, corn, limp strands of elodea. Her coos and burbles greeted an array of freshwater delicacies. She spilled the tray into the water, slurped the tidbits as they floated. Certain fat brown larvae and nymphs, fish roe, certain striped, minnowy fishes engaged her interest. They noted that after she ate, she usually preferred to lounge supine, only her face above the surface, like an otter, rather than perch upright.

Doc Hastings's kids, when they were little, had tried to rescue various wild things over the years—tiny, orphaned cottontails, finches and waxwings defrocked by housecats. Having seen so many failures and successes with the wild ones, he was wary of jumping to conclusions, of ascribing human attributes to the creature. He'd always told the kids, Now, don't get attached. But he tended to think food made her friendly. He thought he saw a smile now and then. Chuck said he'd swear she liked having the company, and added, Once she got used to all of our loud, furry faces.

A few days later, after circumspect petitioning and negotiation, the creature was quietly moved to the shorter of the university's outdoor pools, which was used chiefly for water aerobics and open rec hours, and had the requisite high wooden fence. Her very existence was to be kept on the QT as long as possible; announcements of pool remodeling were posted all over campus. Once over the agitation of her move, the mermaid-thing was curious and not easily startled. At first the roar of loud trucks and jets made her flinch and dive to the bottom, but she quickly learned to ignore such noises.

She made certain high-pitched calls and gurgles at feeding time, certain strange clicks, but it wasn't until the anthropologist brought in a linguist that she showed any interest at all in speech. A word for sun was the first to make her face turn, her eyes glint in recognition. He repeated it; she quickly looked overhead at the sky.

Siouan family: Mandan, Hidatsa, said the linguist.

What's that? Said the biologist.

Tribes of the upper plains. Mostly pushed out by the Lakota, killed by smallpox from the Europeans. Fish? he asked in the same tongue. When he held up a tiny perch fry and repeated it, she just grabbed at the fish. But when he tried an Iroquois language, she repeated the word in a reedy voice, giving what seemed a happy slap of the tail.

A regular My Fair Lady, said Chuck, who was waiting patiently in the hope he'd be allowed to toss minnows in the pool. The royn in Spoyn stoys moynly . . .

She greeted the humans almost eagerly after that. By experimenting with the languages of several indigenous nations, they formed a pidgin with which they could communicate. Then she began to pick up English with astonishing rapidity. She referred to herself as something that sounded like Twee, although the linguists noted a more subtle distinction of vowel, and were unclear whether this were a name, a personal pronoun, or some other part of speech. She quickly learned to say "stop" and "more" during her feedings, "people" when she wanted company, followed by "sleep" and "now." By the end of May, she was at pre-school level speech in English, though she had problems verbalizing concepts of spatial relations, here versus there, back and forward, and possessives. She couldn't seem to grasp tenses of past and present, which caused them some difficulty in communication. Blanchette, a scholar of indigenous languages and an Ojibwe, explained that concepts of time and space didn't exist the same way in such languages. In fact, they found that Twee delineated her sense of time by "sleep" and "swim." The day the heater faltered and the temperature of the pool dropped to 57 she grew agitated, calling Sleep! Sleep! to the expert observing her that afternoon, and scrabbled wildly at the pool's bottom so that her browny-green fingers bled thin blood when she surfaced. The professors concluded that cold had signaled hibernation to her, and she was frantic with the lack of sludge and sediment in the concrete pool. Smooth river rocks, lake-tumbled ovals of basalt and granite, clean sand, were brought in to soothe her.

The graduate students guarding and studying her vied to be her favorites, but Twee didn't seem to form the same kind of attachment; she seemed to have a hard time distinguishing individuals. The biology professor noticed that she relied on hearing far more than sight. As a security measure, her care-takers were given a pattern of code-words to trade with Twee, before feedings and such—she thought it was a new game. She was so trusting, the experts said, that such precautions were necessary.

Twee seemed more at ease once she could communicate. She was even asking to go to her one-time home. They attempted to explain to her that the creek was dead, but she met their remarks with those wide, weed-green eyes and a placid and patient expression. After much debate, they fashioned a special moisture-retaining wrap for her tail, let her lie on a gurney in an ambulance donated for the occasion. She hummed to herself in her whistling way. Once there, anyone peeking through the trees must have thought it was an odd visit by a very tan, sickly patient, with the sheet of the gurney tucked over the tail. It was just after sunrise, and the grass was still dewy; water-striders etched the surface of the creek-bed's few puddles. When they wheeled Twee down to the creek's edge to see its bare, silting bed, she grew quiet. Dead, they explained.

The linguist carefully explained the diverted water—he invoked the mighty beaver for analogy—and how it killed the creek. The sundry experts never could tell much by her facial expression, but Twee seemed thoughtful.

In her characteristic confusion of tenses, she said, I don't stop water. Humans stop water; she snorted audibly through her flat nostrils. She paused and began trying out her new vocabulary, pointing her thin fingers: Tree. Tree. Sun. Bird. She looked down into the creek-bed, made a little whirring sound, a click. Dead, she said.

Word got out almost at once, within two months of the move to the university's pool. Immediately there was great public demand to see this astounding freshwater mermaid. In mid-June, reporters from television stations in Pierre and Bismarck, then from all around the country, were set up with weekly-rental hotel suites. ASTOUNDING FISH-WOMAN FOUND! cackled the tabloids' banner headlines. An Ad-Hoc Twee Care Advisory Committee had been formed, including a famous anthropologist from New York and experts from freshwater aquariums. Offers came rolling in: The Discovery Channel said they'd build Twee a simulated creek of her own, in exchange for rights to round-the-clock video coverage. Revlon wanted a deal in which they'd underwrite Twee's care in exchange for the rights to put her name on a new make-up line in greens and browns; her unusual skin tone would fit with their multiethnic marketing strategy, but they'd have to try focus groups first. These and other ideas came flooding in while various government officials, agencies, think-tanks, and nonprofit foundations tried to figure out who was authorized to speak for Twee. The American Indian Movement weighed in, and the World Wildlife Fund, even UNICEF.

In the meantime, with Twee's permission, the university had opened viewing hours from one to three p.m. on weekends and Wednesdays. The university put security guards outside the gate and at the pool. School officials held meetings to discuss whether certain male visitors were exploiting Twee by ogling her not-very-well developed breasts—but since Twee herself disdained all garments, they decided that as long as the line kept moving, it was okay. By late June they'd discovered they needed to provide a canopy for most of the pool to keep her from sunburn.

Twee put up with the demands of science and publicity with fairly good grace. There was a scare around the Fourth of July when a man hopped the guardrail during viewing hours, and dived into the pool with what looked like a knife. Guards jumped in after him and found it was only a penlight, but after that, they put up a metal detector at the gate in addition to the guards and had 24-hour coverage by biology and veterinary students. The episode unnerved her caretakers more than it did Twee. She seemed to have a high pain threshold, judging from her willingness to submit to blood-drawing for samples; she permitted arm-strength tests from the physical therapists. Even though the experts were falling all over themselves to learn about her anatomy and behavior, the ad-hoc advisory committee figured they didn't want to subject her to the confines of an MRI scanner just yet, not until her English improved to the point where she could really give informed consent. However, she couldn't bear to have the midline portion of her tail touched—she'd twitch and shy away even before contact.

Must correlate to the lateral line in fish, commented Schiffer, the biology professor, An extra sense. She can feel the touch coming through the water.

Fish make up for their peanut brains with some amazing neurology, said the visting Doc Hastings, fanning a hat over his sweating forehead. Sixth sense. I tangled with enough walleye to know that.

Doc Hastings had retired June first and he came by at least once a week, since he wasn't a golfer. He didn't like the line looping around to get a look at Twee in her pool, nor the bleacher seats full of hooting children. He muttered, Poor thing's got no home and barely learned her English and here they got her on show and now all hell's breaking loose. Sometimes he wished the creature had never been found, for her sake. He figured that Twee would like a quiet day in the country even more than he did, it being her native state. The thing belonged with the other mysterious, mud-colored beauties of the plains: the striped earth of Dakota Badlands, yellow-headed blackbirds, Byzantine-patterned rattlers, a beauty as furtive as underground water that made the thrifty prickly pear and grasses bloom. He felt a strange protectiveness, born of his scientific curiosity and an organic sense of the holy in the green creature.

Usually he'd corner one of the graduate students, like humorless Deniece, or Matthew, who staffed the quiet Thursday and Sunday nights, to convey his complaints. Lemme tell you what I know about wild things, he'd begin, or, Have I told you my gramps thought he saw one of these? One day when he was out tilling . . .

Matthew was an earnest, big-eared biology student who preferred to talk physiology with Doc. What did he think about the permeability of her skin? Why skin and not scales above the waist? Could Doc explain to him how her blood chemistry compared to human? What about hemoglobin?

When Matthew wasn't picking his brain, Cassie, an anthropologist-in-training, chased him with a tape recorder in hope of collecting his "folk tales." After all, they held the best hope of capturing any kind of history, she said;

there was so much to learn about Twee since she'd been rescued from the creek bed.

Now that's damn anthropologist talk if you think we rescued her, Doc admonished. Not scientific at all. Don't go thinking we're doing her any favors. She's a wild thing, and nature has her own ways. I'm beginning to think she needs rescuing from us.

I suppose you're right, said Matthew.

Cassie, chastened, nonetheless stuck to the topic of folklore, probed and clarified.

Well, it's not so much folk tales as just things my gramps would tell, and those old-timers, he protested, watching Twee gobble down some small fry. No, he never heard tell of these mermaids seducing farmers and laborers. No, he didn't recall they pointed anyone to hidden springs. I'm sorry to disappoint you, young lady, he said, But the ones I heard was mostly someone catching a glimpse of one sunning on a flat slab of rock. What do you think of those strange eyes of hers? Like to get in there with an ophthalmoscope one of these days; wonder what her retinas look like. Poor mermaid gal, I bet she just wants to be left alone. We don't need to think we know every damn thing in the universe this minute. No, I never heard they were enchanting singers. Now, lemme tell you about wild things . . .

Contrary to Doc Hastings' suppositions, Twee obviously liked to sing; at first, just her own high-pitched calls. The first tune she'd learned, the linguist having a rather juvenile sense of humor and an ill-developed sense of posterity, was "Row, Row, Row Your Boat." She liked to sing with the visiting children. Sometimes she'd have thirty or forty people singing "Row, Row, Row Your Boat." She liked visitors to teach her songs, although when she tried to return the favor, they complained among themselves that she sounded like Yoko Ono at her worst. Of course, the ethnomusicologists came running with their Sony recording equipment.

To the dismay of some of her caretakers, Twee seemed to have something of the performer in her; at the least, she seemed to enjoy visitors' days. Sometimes she liked to play with the balls or diving rings, to breach and splash, antics that delighted the lucky visitors. On a Wednesday afternoon, Twee waved back at the slack-jawed grade-schoolers. She tossed a tennis ball underhand back and forth to them. A funny cackling call seemed her mimicry of their laughter; she also imitated the gurgle of the pool's heater and the bleeping of pagers.

Dr. Virginie Lefèvre, a French behaviorist known for her research on cognition in dolphins, was doing some testing with Twee that day. On this occasion, she was tossing rings. Usually when they played this "game," Twee would wait till they hit bottom, then retrieve them carefully, dropping them into the doctor's waiting palm. Today the expert was trying to see if Twee could conceptualize size—big and small. She'd been coaching Twee on these words with different size rings. Now she threw all three far across the pool. Twee, get only small, she instructed. Twee dived down and retrieved all three. The scientist patiently held up the rings again, leaning over the pool's edge.

Small. Big. Big. Find small, she asked.

Twee pointed to the smaller one.

Yes, she said. Good. Get small. Get only small. Again, she threw all the rings; again, Twee brought them all back, and the children in the stands applauded. Twee glided on her back, clapping along with the excited schoolchildren, who knew how to be an audience much better than how to be scholarly observers.

Hey! yelled a girl in a shirt that said 'Britney', Why don't you train her to jump through hoops? Like the dolphins?

I do not want to train her, said Dr. Lefèvre. This isn't a show—I am a scientist and she's not a pet.

She can't jump as far as an orca, said a boy wearing two baseball caps on top of each other. And she don't sing that good.

An orca is smarter than are you, said the scientist, almost loudly enough.

Kids, be respectful, said their teacher half-heartedly, while she tried to focus her camera on the moving target.

Mon dieu, obviously we must try this when there is *moins* distractions, murmured Lefèvre.

The Sea World people, who also understood audiences, actually wanted Twee to come live with dolphins in a tank. Schiffer, the biology professor, had to explain repeatedly and with fading patience, to successive flunkies who called him, exactly why salt water wouldn't be good for Twee.

She can't just regulate her fluids like an estuarine worm, Schiffer explained; She'd dry out, she'd die. But the pencil-pushers couldn't seem to grasp even this common freshman-level model of marine studies.

The Discovery Channel's proposal also ran into more difficulties when Twee announced to a group of schoolchildren—Mrs. Sundquist's, actually—that she intended to: Go school. She wanted to learn to read, she told the graduate students who habitually scribbled observations about her in lab notebooks. The mayor had a fit when this idea hit the TV news, rightly envisioning the fuss that followed. Private schools publicly offered scholarships. The school superintendent retorted that she could get a fine education in the public schools. Advocates for the differently abled talked about getting her equal access, wheelchairs, and plasticized tail sheaths. For the moment, she was given a tutor, and learned to read using the phonics method in mere weeks. She kept trying to take books and worksheets under water, so they had to be laminated. Chatty news anchors started making smart-dolphin analogies, and Sea World began calling again. By then it was late July. Twee asked if there were any schools in the woods; she said that she missed the trees. They brought in potted ones.

The prairie creature was singing for the visitors, reading her large-print laminate of the abridged *Wind in the Willows*, and a picture book of Native American myths and legends provided by a local AIM member "to remind her of her heritage." She had put on flesh from the diet of fat grubs and slender fish, special algae-based supplements the professors had formulated. Yet she also had somber moods that she declined to explain, when she hovered close to the wall below her trees. Sometimes before sunrise they would find her gliding just below the surface, occasionally making high-pitched calls under water, then into the air; she would pause, as if waiting, then slowly submerge. She didn't respond to them at those times, as if she was swimming in her sleep.

Deniece liked to probe Twee's indigenous vocabulary, showing her flashcards or objects. Whenever she asked how Twee had learned to speak in her own tongue, the creature replied, I hear it—but it was unclear from where or whom. Matthew, the biology student, wrote detailed notes about her movements and diet and occasionally asked Twee if he could take her pulse or temperature. He was both fascinated and repelled by her whiteless eyes and the smooth, featureless slope of scalp around her ear canals. Likewise, Twee found Matthew's noticeable human ears intriguing. It started as curiosity and became a game. She'd order him close to the water, then would poke and pull at his ears with her fingers, which were thinner than a human's. Shell, she'd say, tugging at his ear, Fungus. He imagined her laughing when she did this, but that dynamic of emotion didn't seem to exist in her. He said to Professor Schiffer one day, She's like a housecat; she has moods, she's capable of showing pleasure, fear, pain, familiarity, but I can't imagine her waiting by the door for any master.

Well, she's not domesticated, the professor reminded him, And she's sure not human. We're only beginning to guess what evolutionary processes have shaped her. It's possible she's some sort of bridge species, like a lungfish . . . he mused. That would make her a throwback to the Paleozoic—a missing Mississippian? And yet humans didn't evolve till the Pleistocene epoch; at earliest, Oligocene, when apes developed. She's some sort of relic of the marine era on the plains.

I like to think there's others of her kind, Matthew said. Are there other Twees in the river? Matthew asked her.

One in a river, she replied, Only. She said the same thing or a variant thereof every time he asked, but they could never figure out if she meant each stream only supported one such creature, or whether she was the only one living. Then she'd invariably bring up school. She'd say, Twee go school. Lots peoples, lots childrens: school.

Matthew hesitated to tell the professor that he thought school was her idea of company; after all, he was probably imposing human behavior onto her again. But he wondered if hers was a social species, if she missed her companions.

Deniece hadn't found a Tweeish translation for *school.*

Besides school, she wanted big water, she told them. She wanted big trees. They taught her to call that concept *Home*. Then they reminded her of what she'd seen on her trip to the dry creek-bed, moist only after rains, the surface mud cracking into pancakes that curled at the edges as it dried. Dead. Home.

In the absence of weighty news from Wall Street, a standout summer movie, or an outbreak of world peace, the discovery of the prairie mermaid had spawned a national mania. Around the state, small boys and girls, grown men and women with no particular interest in animal behavior, bought hip-waders and began churning up creek beds with coal-shovels and garden rakes, looking for silted brown forms. The department of natural resources got emergency funding from the legislature to hire more rangers and staff to patrol waterways, since the scavengers were stirring up silt and even old sludge-oil deposits, tainting drinking water and causing fish-kills. Anglers were grumpy, and the *TIME* magazine cover of Twee only spurred the frenzy. Meanwhile, the university licensed the production of rubbery, floating figurines of Twee, Twee T-shirts and travel tumblers, the recording "Songs of the Mermaid" to help support the cost of her care until things could be decided.

The federal government was still grappling with whether Twee's status and rights should be considered as Indigenous People or under the Endangered Species Act and which agency should have jurisdiction over her fate. Amnesty International, concerned that she was being held without consent, sent a senior investigator to interview her. No, she was content, she explained, with a little help from Deniece—she missed Home, but since the water had stopped running, there was no life for her there—some day she might like bigger water. And *School.* Amnesty International met with the Sierra Club about legal challenges, while the Department of the Interior held endless hearings. In August, an official board of trustees made up of various scientific and cultural experts—including the biologist but not the linguist—was appointed to safeguard her welfare. Doc Hastings read about the trustees in the paper and commented aloud to the spirit of dear departed Mrs. Hastings over breakfast, as he often did on perplexing matters, that this was a fine kettle of fish, pardon the pun, for the poor mermaid gal; you couldn't help but feel a bit sorry for her, like a stray fox on a golf course or something. It's just not right, he muttered over his whole-wheat toast, Like making a fox into a house-dog. Later on, he and Chuck would hatch schemes for the betterment of Twee's life over the back fence before adjourning for a beer and a shot.

All the press coverage and the Amnesty International challenge brought in the animal-rights activists. It started with a few picketers sporting "Free Twee" placards in front of the university, letters to the editor. One of the grad students was secretly a sympathizer. It was on a moonless night that he fogged the cameras, sent Neil the security guard to investigate his report of a damaged lock, so the van could sidle past the emergency exit of the basketball arena and around to the pool. He told Twee they were taking her to school. Twee was delighted, as far as one could tell—she sang one of her shrieky tunes and they helped her out onto a rubberized tarp, which was smeared with some kind of gel to protect her scales, then wrapped around her thick, flat, brown tail. She told them of her trip to the creek. The student sang with her in the back of the van and laughed. They traveled for about an hour, then the van backed down a paved boat ramp, toward the river.

Alder grew thickly over the banks next to the ramp; current fractured the surface of the broad river into gray flint, obsidian. The three of them stood next to the van and waved their arms enthusiastically. There, they said gleefully to Twee, you wanted bigger water, you are free—but she didn't understand *free*, didn't understand the game. When they slid her out of the van and she caught sight of the dark slide of the water, the churn of its current, she asked warily, School? And they laughed and said, no, bigger water. A nice big river.

No, I want go school, she said, still having problems with her infinitives and verb tenses. I want read, I want books, I want school with childrens.

It's okay, explained Matthew, the biology student; it's clean water, no dioxin, no phosphate overload, lots of fish, larvae. Here, I'll go in with you. It's okay.

They carried her down to the river and gently unfurled the tarp, slid her into the cool water. Matthew walked in up to his shorts to reassure her. She slipped out from under his hand.

Now you're free, he said again, and the others around him beamed and repeated it, Free, free. Your new home, they said.

But Twee clenched her hands down into the mud, heaved herself half onto the ramp, wincing as her sensitive tail scraped on the rough concrete. Home. Dead, she said. She glowered at the river. Stop, she told them, a word she knew well. Dead. Stop. Too big. Stop.

I know this is sudden, Matthew said, but it had to be a surprise. It's what you wanted. Bigger water. More.

She's just having separation anxiety, said one of his cohorts, a girl with shrubby red brows and hair. It's to be expected. Stockholm syndrome: She's identified with her captors. She has to learn to fend for herself again.

She belongs in the wild. I'll miss her, said Matthew, wading from the water, But I'll be glad she has her freedom. He sniffled back his tears.

Twee slid low into the water, clinging along the bank.

They threw her a handful of mayfly nymphs and fish and they left her there, submerged up to her neck beside the boat ramp, looking out at the swift, dark current. They couldn't see her hidden profile as they pulled away, couldn't hear while they were singing and congratulating themselves and saying that surely now they'd earned a trip to England to liberate some captive mink.

She stayed there long after the van left. The river was cold. It looked black and flinty, purposeful in its lunge to a far-away sea. With her chin in the water, Twee let out one of her strange, high-pitched cries, waited without a reaction. She slipped under the water and crept close to the bank, surfaced beneath the outstretched arms of the alder, hesitated. Then, working her long tail against the current, she began her halting way upstream.

The One Thing I'm Good At

Another farewell lunch. The good Thai restaurant has become our spot for department rituals—birthdays, showers—they make a passable chicken hot basil. Close to three years, this time. Outside, I lingered on the sidewalk, clutching my parting gifts—the bunch of cello-wrapped mums, book, picture frame—exchanging best wishes, slow to leave. My boss used to tease, call me his Girl Lieutenant so that I could correct, Woman Lieutenant. He hates goodbyes, disruptions, but he meant it when he said I will be *a tough act to follow*. So why do I feel like I'm losing my touch?

I leave better than anyone else—they all say so. Of course they're always *happy for my good fortune*—a hand fidgets on a desk blotter—disappointed, perhaps, *but sounds like a great opportunity*—twitching a pencil. In the end, they are impressed and nostalgic, *what a good egg*. Roomy shoes for the next slob to fill. I am never more appreciated than after I give my ample six-week notice, after I vanish.

My annual reviews are cross-hatched with firm black rows of checks—*competent, above average*—and it's not bragging to say I do my job well. *Shows initiative—accepts assignments willingly and completes them responsibly—works well with a variety of co-workers?* Check. *Contributes in a meaningful way to the department team?* Check. And when I go, there are files neatly arranged in the desk I will leave behind, tidy manila folders labeled "work in progress," "key procedures," and a helpful exit memo for my successor. So professional. That's why I always get the lunch and flowers. Sometimes I even keep in touch.

Perhaps it's because I'm not attached, do not fear displacement. This means I can get to work instead of working to get ahead. *Work completed on time and effectively*. I am good-humored, I lunch with my office-mates, twenty-something, datebooked, on the go. I blend in without having to try. Sometimes I stick around long enough that they start talking promotion. It's that Peter principle: they promote you from things you're good at into jobs you can't figure out, can't handle. I like to feel on top of my tasks, not of the totem pole. When they start talking like that—new duties, responsibilities—it means time to move on. Why set yourself up for failure?

I leave more easily than anybody else. My expectations glide along at ground level. After we're done I get dressed in the dark and slip out the door quickly, without a fuss. I say, Shh, don't get up, and the man drowsing in the bed, whatever his name is, breathes fondly after me, grateful that I understand his body's post-coital inertia, the best possible finale; *what a gal.*

During those months when something drags on, turns into a weekly gig, I keep my balance. I have no flair for acrimony, greed, or guilt. I don't leave suitcases full of makeup, a jungle of nylons, in his apartment—just toothbrush and shampoo, disposables. Don't steal T-shirts or fill up his voice-mail or his calendar. I leave plenty of space. And when my lover says that, during the last three or four weeks of sex, movies, and dinners, he's really been thinking *we'd be better off as friends*, I pause over my hot-and-sour soup—*oh, I see*—finish the meal, walk to my car, and only then do I perhaps react, breathing clouds of something the flavor of annoyance or blame, often self-directed, into the windshield. Later, I toss out his toothbrush and shaving cream, drop off the polar-fleece jacket, book, and bike pump in his front hallway, quietly, without a note. I go for a long run. I do not call the answering machine repeatedly and hang up. I do not rehash the situation. I do not call late at night in a drunken fit of sobbing. I have not allowed reasons for tears. I do not sob.

And when, after the third date with the guy from the party who still evokes no chemistry, I politely decline the next offer, I also explain that *I guess I'm just not ready* or maybe that *it's not you, I'm all over the map after my breakup*, all carefully shouldering my lack of interest—*responsible, congenial, professional, taking the initiative*—check.

Not good at: cooking. Not good at Christmas cards. Not at all good at householding in its various fashions. Not particularly good at fashion (*average*), but very good at ruthlessly cleaning out the closet. Not good at small lies necessary for maintenance of human relations. Not good at bridge, taxes, family folklore, anything requiring dedication of complex rules to memory. Not good at games, except checkers and Othello, red-and-black, black-and-white.

Good at: declining the annual invitations—weddings, birthdays, congratulations *Shh It's a SURPRISE*—of acquaintances who can't be bothered with me the rest of the year. Good at maps, strategies, navigation. Good at quick starts: fast out of the gate, begin my jog at a too-quick pace and pull up later, winded, enjoying the sensation of speed, outdistancing, of autonomy, motion. Good at leaving home, on my brief, annual visits to the family. Changing hairdos and hair color. I politely say, No, not interested, and hang up so the telemarketer can get on to the next prospect. Good at impromptu adventures. Efficient at moving my life across the city, up and down stairs. Wrapping breakables and notifying the post office of *my change of postal address in a timely manner*. It's probably time to shift across state lines again. Leaving, it's the one thing I'm good at—they all say so.

So why am I losing my touch for early departures; why do I hang around, cling a moment longer and yet hate the delay? Tell me why it suddenly feels dishonest to slip out from the sheets in the reflected glow of the city night and say, no really, I have to. I dawdle. I never felt so chatty before, *wanted to see how, just wanted to hear*, I force my hand from the phone before I can dial, want to slap myself. Strange greeds, for time and presence, arise in me. Horrified, the day I realized I'd left my old sneakers and a couple of CDs over there. The fact that I appear to be—what?—getting *comfortable* makes me *nervous*, sensations that grow in counterpoint to each other, *slap, slap*, bickering. Want to reclaim those absent powers, step back onto that path my feet have worn familiar, *hit the trail*, pound the strange reactions right out of my blood with a good, hard run.

I think perhaps I've gotten sloppy, inconsiderate. Forgotten to maintain boundaries. Maybe creating a situation that might be on my conscience. Taking up space. At your warm side, tangled in the blankets, I catch myself making plans, making assumptions, a scent of continuity. Tell me why your breathing feels like part of my bed, why the norm of night has shifted. Your skin, your face, like a memory I'd forgotten, returned, with a sudden ache for having missed it. Flowers from my office-mates on the nightstand. When I quit, you didn't even flinch. It has not occurred to you I'm capable of other flights.

I am noticing what it feels like to *stay*, but by your side, I suddenly want to bolt, the usual, the familiar; want to sprint down the street, around the corner, shoes slapping heavy on pavement and my lungs huffing. Want to hop in the car and follow only a map, some reddened interstate arteries. Then you'll see. Then I'll really be worth knowing. I'm so good, so graceful, so complete at leaving, everyone says so. You'd see me at my best. The one thing I'm good at. But if I want to stay—if I learn how to stay—it might *be a great opportunity* but I do it so clumsily, I have no compass for it, my marks inevitably will be *fair–average–poor.* An effort, a prayer: *trying.* I am trying just to breathe with your breathing, but I'm halting, I stutter, I want to lace my sneakers, limber up and go. Then nobody's pace to match but my own. It is so, so easy to fail, and I hate being a beginner.

Bad Hand

It went like this: Dane would go to the gas station mini-mart on County Road C but never fill the car quite full. Or he would stop there for coffee—not every morning, but a couple of times a week. Dane would nose around the junk food or finger the vivid *USA Today* till any other customers were out of the way. Then he'd edge over to the counter, venture some remark on weather or the bad wreck on I-94 to the wispy-haired girl at the register, crease the felted dollars in one hand and wait for her response. Her name was Janine.

Cute, he thought the first time, her distracted stare out the window at the service plaza. One day, he was finally brave enough to use the name pinned to her smock, introduced himself. She had marvelous posture. An egg-shaped face with a pointed chin; soft, sandy-brown hair that tended to drift, like leaves or grass, over her eyes or ears. She had opinions on things. Now he was hooked and suffered sudden mood swings if she wasn't there. Her hands were long: oval palms, tapering fingers, with the knuckles just a little big, fluttering around the buttons of the register, her collar. She plunged in and out of shyness, sometimes waited for him to speak first. It got to where she would say "Hi, Dane! How's it going?" or he would compliment her on her earrings, and they would talk a bit, till a customer came in or a silence made him suddenly self-conscious and he would flush and stutter, slip away, bad hand cowering in his pocket.

Dane lost the right thumb and pointer when he'd tried to grab Rory from between the boxcars—Rory had lost his left leg below the knee. Now the left hand did all the opening, gripping, prying, pinching, while the right was downgraded to punching buttons, pushing swing-doors, shading eyes from sun. The loss of Dane's fingers was bad all the way around, but it was complicating the situation with the girl. He'd had some bad luck with his bad crushes, and he hadn't even asked her out yet. He was 29 years old and it was ridiculous, but there he was, paralyzed.

This had been going on for two whole months.

Before the accident, Rory and Dane didn't hang out together much—the occasional beer or bowling with the other guys after work at the elevator. Dane thought Rory a little too loud, too crass, his opinions nudging into nosiness. If not opposites, they were mirror images—Dane darker with lank brown hair, legs a tiny bit too short, broad planks instead of high cheekbones, a slightly bulbous nose; Rory blonde and red-faced, hawk-nosed, old-chicken thin and tough. Dane liked music, movies, and baseball, and Rory preferred stock-car racing, pro wrestling, and cursing back at AM talk radio. Afterwards, whether it was some handshake of blame and gratitude, something had cemented them into a bar-stool kind of friendship, a comparison of recoveries, bandages, painkillers. They hid out together, getting used to their reshaped and faltering bodies. Rory and Mary Jo started asking Dane over to dinner; they watched the races and ball games at home, removed from staring eyes.

"Dane, you gotta just ask her out or it's never going nowhere," said Mary Jo, clearing dishes from a table padded with Rory's NASCAR fiftieth-anniversary place mats. "You got a fifty-fifty shot. You have talked to her, haven't you?"

"Oh, yeah. Sure."

Rory laughed and went to the fridge for another beer. "He's all talk."

Mary Jo was trying to quit smoking, which made others' personal problems even more attractive to her. "Well, does she smile at you?"

Dane pictured that sweet smile, almost shy, though he didn't tell Mary Jo as she swept crumbs from the table with short, neat fingers.

"Awright," said Rory, popping open a beer for Dane. "Hell, she's probably crying to her girlfriends how come you haven't asked her out yet." He wiped foam from his blond mustache.

"Yeah, well, it's just—timing," Dane said. It had been a while since a girl had caught his eye. He slumped over his beer.

"Geez, Dane," snorted Mary Jo, pushing her big glasses up the bridge of her nose. "You look like a man thinking on a death sentence. Gloom is coming off you in waves."

"You weren't like this with that last one," Rory said. "That brunette, you know."

"Carla," Dane muttered. They'd met in a bar and it went straight to the bedroom. No moonjunespoon romance.

"Yeah, she was a live wire, nice lookin', too. Aw, don't look at me that way, honey, you know I like 'em old and sassy," he teased, slapping at his wife's behind as she loaded the dishwasher.

Dane had always been a little shy, so he had a history of desperate, furtive crushes. But he'd had girlfriends that lasted, too; had even talked about marrying Janet, his high school sweetheart. He'd liked Carla, her gap-toothed smile, her confident, companionable body—but it was off as quickly as it had started, no colicky recriminations. Now he just wanted to change the subject.

Mary Jo sat down, her finger twirling a pen instead of an after-dinner cigarette, and fixed him with her eye. "Just get it over with, Dane."

"I know, I know, but she's got a big reason to say no." He waggled his orphan digits.

"Love stinks," agreed Rory cheerfully. He excelled at the obvious, often loudly calling the play after the announcer. "It'll give you an ulcer but what you gonna do? It shouldn't matter—if she shoots you down, you're on your way."

"Right," Dane said. "So, is it a night race this week?" He thought, I'm done for. It matters. His left hand drummed on the table, *Taps*.

It was a cool, late spring, time of anxious waiting: farmers, equipment salesmen, elevator managers, everyone with one eye on the sky, worried about too much rain or too little, a late frost. Dane excused his procrastination by telling himself he was too busy for such foolishness. Unlike Rory he was back at work, overseeing the loading of the train cars that bellied up to the large grain elevator to fill with tons of corn, oats, whatever came hissing down the chute. In season, huge "unit trains" of a hundred cars—an endless cycle of emptying and filling. The work was not as dangerous as the quarry but not safe, either. Just the year before, an elevator had exploded in Nebraska, and three men were killed—buried alive, suffocated in a sluice of hard durum. Every day Dane saw how the sheer aggregate weight of things that piece by piece were nothing, grains that could be winnowed in air—flecks of barleycorn, wheatberry—could pile up to a crushing power, grains of sand that, fired together, become pounds of molten glass.

It had happened in a big swirl of grain dust last fall. Rory had been up on top of the boxcars, popping the hatches, and Dane tried to catch him as he fell toward the coupling; Dane's hand no match for the hardware and tonnage of a car fully loaded with seed corn. Rory took a bad twist and Dane's hand was crushed, arteries and veins beyond mending. Doctors had trimmed their stumps neatly. They left Dane a slight concavity where thumb once met wrist, reset the other two fingers (the pinky was fine) and put him in a cast, big bandages.

Their accident, as Dane thought of it, demanded strange accommodations. Rory had a beige and hairless fake leg he stumped around on; only a mild stiffness at the knee made him look gimpy. Rory had been an obnoxious weekend drunk but now was strangely purposeful. He was still on workman's comp and in a county training program to learn computers. Dane was going through a clumsy period of translation; it seemed his brain slowly hand-carried certain messages from one side to the other, rather than sending an electric pulse. Dane had been a rightie but now he had the handwriting of a child with his untrained left. He started buying beer and pop in cans—easy to open one-handed, as long as you have a thumb. A missing thumb was a hindrance. He asked Rory, Wasn't that what separated apes and man from the rest of the creatures? It was true, Rory said; you got left with a paw, a flipper. Dane thought of it that way too, the claw, a devil-hand, barring his way to Janine.

She had never seen him whole-handed. Dane's hands were not pretty. Working hands—hard calluses, blisters, nails that never quite shed their grime, despite gritty pumice soap and nail brush. The rest of him wasn't so rough. He thought he had a prayer, if he kept the paw out of the way. She seemed friendly enough, but maybe friendly was as far as she cared to go. Dane had no way to know if she thought about him the way he thought about her, every single night; nights when his desires got the better of him and he conjured different scenarios of being with her, always picturing he had ten fingers that gently discovered her skin, or imagining her voice in those quiet moments before sleep. He knew he was only filling in gaps of what he didn't know but liked so well.

With Rory and Mary Jo teasing and bossing, Dane set himself a date to ask Janine out and proceeded to lose sleep until the day of reckoning. He got a haircut, a new scent of Speed Stick; tossed and turned, as if the asking were the date itself, and not the starting point. He rehearsed it and rehearsed it. Then he was afraid he'd rehearsed it too much and he'd get stuck. He wasn't used to advice, and it addled him.

"Don't say *sometime*," Mary Jo had instructed from a bar-stool. She was driving him nuts. "Otherwise it's too easy to slip past. Ask her out for a specific time, and if she wants to, she'll be damn sure to let you know. No apologies, no excuses, don't fish around. And Christ, Dane, don't forget to smile."

Rory just made some crack about first base, second base.

Dane picked out a decent-looking shirt and did his best job on the stubborn fingernails. He fussed and fidgeted with his hair, his collar, for so long that he could no longer tell one adjustment from the next. He followed Mary Jo's advice in front of his mirror, a starched grin. Janine was alone in the store; his three fingers in the jacket pocket fidgeting as best they could without a thumb to worry, he just took a deep breath, hung his head and said it:

"Janine, I really like talking to you and I uh—wondered if you'd like to go out to dinner this weekend." His eyes caught hers, then cast down to the counter, where her fingers twirled a twist-tie. The coffee unfurled its steam on the counter.

"Oh," she said; she hesitated and finally he had to look up, see the moment of struggle in her face. He was about to say, "It's okay, forget it," quick to bow out and foam over the fiery mess when she said, "I'd like that very much." He looked up again and her face was blushy, and she flicked the drifting strands from her eyes. He struggled to keep the cheesy grin from splitting wider on his face; stared at the gasoline additives instead to get his bearings.

"Um. How about Saturday at six? I could pick you up—or here if you'd prefer, or we could meet, if that's better—"

She paused. Pulled a strip of tape out of the register and jotted on it. "I guess it's okay if you pick me up. Here's the address. It's the first side street after Sherwin-Williams paints on Washington."

Dane folded it between the good fingers, carefully into the shirt pocket, quickly memorized the last name in case—God forbid—he lost it. "Great. Great. I'm looking forward to it." Out of the store, in a daze.

Dane's remaining right fingers, pinky, ring and middle, had started to acquire new abilities of their own. They worked more independently than before, when they had been a welded unit. The pinky cleaned an irritant from his eyelid, the former middle finger punched buttons on the phone, redistributed mustard on a frankfurter, and ring finger was good for planing and gripping in tandem with a fellow digit. They were regaining confidence, curiosity. But it was still hard to brush his teeth with his left hand—the fine-tuning was off. Dane now wore his watch on his right because he needed a thumb to close the clasp. Fingers fumbled with shirt buttons, one-handed; still so awkward, he worried he wouldn't be able to touch a woman with any effectiveness, that way. And would she shudder if he brushed back the hair from her face with those rough, lonesome leftovers?

He combed his hair one way then another, shaved carefully with his meandering left. Liberal doses of Cornhuskers' lotion on the rough calluses. When he rang the bell, Janine did not invite him in, but slid out and locked the door behind her. She smiled, warm but a little shy. "I thought we'd go to Callahan's," he said. "They have really good beef, unless you don't like meat, and then we could go someplace else." He opened the car door, hoped she wasn't a tofu-eater, though he told himself it was a small thing, he could get used to it.

"That sounds nice," Janine said, buckling her seat belt. She gave a happy sigh. "This is really nice."

They got a booth and the seat was a little low for her. She wore a blue dress and little sparkling earrings that she played with, fidgeting slender fingers with their slightly big knuckles. He realized he'd never seen her before without the checkered smock, and he told her so and they laughed and he said she looked nice and she said thank you, so do you. She wasn't tiny, a healthy average girl, maybe a little more in the hips than he'd been able to tell behind the counter, but in no way unpleasant.

"Order anything you want," he said. He got the prime rib. He had learned how to wedge the fork soundly between middle and ring finger so he could cut his meat. She ordered the surf and turf special. Dane mostly kept his bad hand in his lap and midway through dinner he said, "I'll save you the trouble of asking, you've always been so polite about it, but I lost those fingers in an accident." He had rehearsed this so it wouldn't sound like he was stupid or careless, but not like he was bragging, either. "A guy fell between the cars and I was trying to catch him and we both got caught."

"I'm real sorry," she said. "But you seem to manage really well. You'd hardly notice." She smiled slightly.

He was glad she didn't get all concerned, though her voice was adequately sympathetic.

He found out she had grown up in Redwood Falls with two sisters, played clarinet in the marching band. He told her where he worked and about his brother Tim in the Air Force. Janine rapped the table edge, eyes bright; she had a weakness for air shows. He actually had a funny story that didn't make him look too bad, about trying to bowl with his left hand. At some point she excused herself and he watched her walk to the back, that great posture like her shoulders held the sky, those hips adding some curve to the blue dress. But he could tell by the sliver of her skimming past the intervening wall that she stood at the pay phone, and something scrabbled at his stomach. Who on earth could she be calling? Calm down, he thought; she seems to be having fun. Maybe her mother, or a girlfriend; a buddy system, so they know he's not a psycho-killer. His mood suddenly swung to compassion; the risk in getting into a strange man's car. She came smiling back to the table.

He said, "I probably should have arranged to meet you, instead. I forget that it must make you nervous, going out with someone you don't really know. I mean . . ."

She blinked. "Oh. No. It's fine. I mean, I feel like I know you. Say, do I know you?" she teased, smiled, toyed with the earring. "Aren't you the fellow with the coffee?" They laughed. She finished all the shrimp and left half the steak on her plate. He was liking new things about her; the slope of her forearm, and her eyes, a little narrow and bright, hazel.

Turned out that they liked a couple of the same country-western bands. Janine didn't know much about baseball, but that was okay. They'd been in the same shopping mall during the tornado of '97 that knocked off the end of the movie multiplex. Dane's stomach was full and happy; hope started to make itself comfortable.

The fateful moment. Walked her to her door but he was nervous, she was nervous; she stepped a pace back and beamed at him, said, "I had a really, really nice time, Dane," and he asked if she'd like to try it again sometime and she said yes. She rushed a quick peck to his cheek then slipped inside the door. His heart felt wine-drunk, sopping, generous, singing. What's there to like so much? he asked, but it kept thumping, I don't know but I do, I do, I do.

Dane drove home in a giddy stupor. When he washed his face, some idiot grinned back in the mirror. This was stupid because he barely knew her. He was like a gambler feeding silver to a one-armed bandit, hooked on a dream. It gave him physical pangs and twinges, and made him keener on the romantic country songs—and broken-hearted ones, too. Better than plain lust, and worse. He wondered if she was the cotton-panty type or more into lacy things; somehow he always pictured the former. He hadn't even kissed her; maybe the feel of her in his arms would be all wrong. It was a big old grade-school crush, hope and doubt, that's what it was. And if she said no, he knew he'd continue to obsess despairingly for a while until he mourned that loss of hope-dread rush.

Shit, Dane thought, I haven't learned a damn thing since high school.

When Dane stopped by the store on Tuesday, Janine was animated and smiling, bright with nervous chat. Giddy, he had to let a few tracers of small talk whistle past before he asked her out for a second date, and she said, "I can't this weekend, I'm sorry . . . but can we go some other time?" For a moment he felt a crushing squeeze, his flipper-hand twitched in his pocket; then her last words seeped in, and he rallied. So he picked her up on a Thursday and they went to the movies. He sat on her right and during the scary parts her hand grazed and settled on his whole left, and her touch was barely warm, not cool. He couldn't tell if it was shampoo or some light perfume she wore that smelled flowery and faintly spicy and desperately made him want to kiss her neck below the wispy strands. Afterward he asked if she wanted to get a cup of coffee, and Janine leaned into him, her head almost resting on his shoulder, then pulled away, sighing. "I can't, I really should get home." As they neared her apartment she became quiet; her face solidified. She hopped quickly out of the car and said "Sorry I have to run—don't get out—thank you, it was lovely. Really. Come see me this week, okay?" She vanished into her apartment.

What was that? A brush-off? he thought. No kissing there. But she'd asked him to pop in at work . . . . Had he done something wrong? He wasn't one for grabbing and pawing; her hand had sought his, his good hand, in the darkness.

Dane tossed in his bed. He knew he wasn't being realistic. All he had were little pieces of Janine piling up, making a gleaming, loving, happy image of Janine as he wished her—Janine in the park, Janine in his bed—a character that was only half-true, since he couldn't grasp her, really, not yet.

Given the situation, he didn't want to be too pushy, or too standoffish. When he leaned on the counter, asked her out for Saturday night, he said, "Would you mind giving me your phone number? Not that I don't like seeing you in person, especially in your lovely—uh, smock," and laughed at his own ease.

Her face flashed briefly furtive, looking at the horoscope scrolls at the checkout, then clearing. She said, "I've been having some problems with my phone lately. Why don't I call you on Friday and we can firm up plans?" She handed him a stick pen and a discarded lottery ticket and he wrote in his wobbly childish scrawl. Back to the car, off to work; a yes? But no phone? On the radio, he couldn't decide—the darker country songs, or the ones about true love? Where were the songs about trucks and dogs and highways when he needed them? He switched to an all-news station.

Doubt was piling up; he could call up no memory of confidence, romances before he was damaged goods. Dane nearly ruined the third date with his mood. Janine slid away from her plate to use the phone again, and when she came back he was torn between the thing he didn't want to call love pulsing in him, and realizing that he didn't know her, didn't really know her at all, but knew something was amiss. She was there, right across from him—clearly attracted, smiling, the blush that flickered at times, the slight brushes her clean white hands gave to his good hand, his arm, his shoulder, the flirtations she bravely threw him then backed away from. Yet retreat seemed housed in her straight-backed frame. She hadn't seemed that unnerved by his hand, but perhaps there it was, fear of the cripple. Maybe it wasn't the paw, but him. Or something else in her? Her little evasions of word and body.

He pulled out the chair for her and she sat, replaced the cloth napkin in her lap. "Is everything okay?" he asked, taking his seat.

"Why do you ask?" she returned his gaze evenly.

"Oh, nothing. Do you want coffee or dessert?"

"Hmmm. I will if you will."

He had gone heavy, matter-of-fact, and he wasn't sure she'd noticed.

At her home, he got out, walked around, opened the passenger door. He stepped in close, half with desire and half with grim-faced determination, to kiss her goodnight. She leaned in, he got a whiff of that sweet scent, and her lips pressed back to his, parted, he felt the smooth tip of her tongue—abruptly pulled away as she faltered, turned to kiss his cheek instead. "Thanks," she said. "I'm—thanks. I had a great time. I have to go." She smiled, apologetically or warmly, slipped inside her door, leaving him with a ghost of pressure on his lips and lurching stomach.

The next day Dane picked his way along the row of seats in the grandstand, trying not to spill. The method involved his third finger sticking down into his own cup of beer, and he handed the good cup to Rory. Mary Jo had stayed home; she was into stock cars but thought the tractor-pulls were a huge bore. It was early May, and the mud was real. The super stock tractors were getting organized, and a haze of exhaust hovered in the ring, giving the air an acrid tang that reached the bleachers.

"This here guy in the red cab, he won up at Theresa, Wisconsin, back last year," Rory said. He was chatty. He'd installed and ripped out circuit boards all the previous day at the training center and hadn't made a single mistake, as he'd announced at least twice. "Hey, did you know they added street stock semi-trucks to the Wisconsin State Championship pull? I might have to go on up there this year. But if you want to go you got to tell me soon, only mail order tickets."

Dane shook his head, laughing. "Where do you get all of this stuff?"

"You wouldn't believe, they got all of this on the Internet now." Dane looked down on the mud track as the first driver was fiddling with his hitch, inspecting the chain.

Rory took a drink, squinted at Dane. "That girl of yours didn't want to come?"

Dane's feet jittered on bleachers and his lonesome digits trailed circles on his leg. "Didn't ask. I don't know. Why can't anything be straightforward?"

Rory busted out laughing. "You expect anything with women to be straightforward? Nope. NASCAR, maybe. Or baseball. Not women." He seemed very amused by himself.

Dane had no regrets over what he'd done for Rory–not the desperate grab, the action itself. The act was born there in his body and waiting, without the benefit of thought. He was angry, regretted the loss of his thumb, but knew he couldn't have done otherwise. That impulse was inevitable, just like loving Janine. Or whatever he felt. His body had made it without his mind, of a moment.

Dane ran all five through his hair, worrying it into clumps. "I know she likes me, but she's hiding something. She won't give me her phone number, she's never once let me in the door, not even a peep; she's always waiting when I pull up. I'm wondering if there's someone else in the picture." He sighed, turned his beer cup on his knee.

"Whoa, jack, whoa," Rory said. "This is what happens when you get stuck on one so quick instead of shopping around. Didn't I tell you?" He shifted his fake foot on the plank beneath him. "First of all, if she was taking you as something on the side, she never, ever would have let you pick her up at home. That's just stupid, man. Maybe she's embarrassed of where she lives. She can't be making much at a mini-mart." He turned back to the track.

"There's another idea occurred to me." Dane took a pull at his beer. "I'm wondering maybe she has a kid. That she's afraid to tell me."

Rory's smile slackened. "Hmm, yeah. That's a heavy deal to lay on someone, you know, that baggage. Complicates things."

"It's only a problem if she's going to lie about it, make it into a problem."

"Alls I mean is, you feel like you gotta be serious if there's a kid involved and all that. Can't just have fun and see how it goes. You know."

Dane downed the rest of his draft. In the oval below, the cab was hitched up and ready to roll. They watched as the tractor lurched forward then halted with a jerk as the chains went taut. For a second or two it held motionless though the tires churned, straining against the dead weight. Dane knew what that felt like.

"But here's the thing," he said, "this paw. Maybe she's afraid of this thing, my touch. They see this hand here, and who wouldn't be grossed out?" He grimaced.

"Aw, don't go looking for trouble. You got the sense she likes you, then she likes you. Maybe she's playing hard to get or something." Rory consulted the oracle of the oval as the truck labored forward. "God, you're a sorry cuss. You should be all happy, she ain't turned you down yet. Look at you, a mess, and you haven't got no sugar yet." He laughed.

"Shut the hell up," Dane said. "Some help you are. What do you—you were already married when you got mashed up, Mary Jo's just glad you're alive. Most people can't even tell from looking you got a prosthetic leg. Me, it's obvious. What woman's gonna want that?"

Rory shot him a sideways sneer, wedged his beer cup between his fake and real feet. "Now you're just being sorry for yourself. Don't think I got off so easy. You're the one making up problems. I can't help you none. Shut up and watch the trucks."

Days piled up slowly. Dane waited all the way to Thursday to go into the mini-mart. A whole week. Just to prove he could do it. If she dropped him like a rock that very day, he could get past it; he didn't need to see her. "Janine" was just something he'd cooked up in his own head, a little phantom to keep him company, her face pasted on his fantasy. He waited for a Subaru to pull out of the station before he went inside.

"Hi," he said, nodding, hands shoved into jacket pockets.

"Hi," she said; an uncertain smile. "Um—haven't seen you all week. I guess you've been busy?"

He nodded affirmative, anxiously taking in the beef jerky display, the cans of chaw, Lifesavers. Awful quiet.

"Hey—are you mad at me about something?" she said softly. Her face had flattened and her fingers spidered around the counter top. "I've been racking my brain for what I did wrong; I can tell it's something, and I just don't know what." Perplexed, almost brave, down-turned mouth.

"No. Why, no, I'm not mad. I guess—I guess I was just reacting to—how you were acting to me." Somebody came in for pump number seven and Dane stepped aside, waited as she rang up the sale, for the bell on the door to ring in closing. Scanned cartons of cigarettes up above for answers. He inhaled. "I'm not asking for any kind of explanation, 'cause your business is your business, and you can tell me what you see fit. Maybe it's me, maybe you think of me—as a cripple or something . . . but there's something in you holding back, and—" She blinked, slow. He hated the baldness of the question: "I'm asking, do you want to keep seeing me?"

Janine stopped her hand in its path. Reached up behind her own neck, rubbed it, in some gesture of comfort, let her hand fall. He felt the seconds sifting down around him, one by one, weighted. "Dane." She looked him in the eye, earnest, cheeks flushing, fingertips smoothing the counter. "It's nothing about you—I do want to see you. I like you an awful lot." She paused; her voice lowered. "You said you don't need explanations. If you really mean that . . . I don't feel like making any right now, not yet. If you can stand to trust me—I mean, I want to see you." She exhaled; now she was tense, tentative. "There, now it's your turn, or you can head for the hills if you want."

He wasn't sure what to say, didn't dare sound false. He nodded, okay.

She wouldn't look up. Tensed, coiled behind the counter, behind her drifting hair, her neck waiting for the blow, and he could see her strength and fragility entwined, how she steeled herself in the midst of it, the way glass can bake in the earth or soak in the sea for centuries without corroding, but shatter at an impact. She was struggling, too; she was not going to let herself cry. Damn it, he thought, why is it all so difficult?

"Listen, maybe when I pick you up on Saturday, we could just play it by ear." He leaned an elbow on the counter, made her look up.

Janine breathed, twitched a smile, faintly. He wasn't sure what the question was but he knew how to answer it, and he took her oblong right in his good left, soothed the smooth back of her hand with his thumb. He kept the deformed paw in his pocket, for now. He let out a big exhalation. "I'm sorry I'm so bad at this," he said. "What a mess." She laughed, almost like a cry.

That night at home, Dane listened to the radio while he washed his few dishes. The refrain whined on, something about missin' you, and he found himself getting irritated at the nasal yelp. Exhaustion buried him like sand. All the hours and minutes he spent pining over this girl who made him light up, made him despair, whom he barely knew, all the doubt and excitement warring in him till he was wrung out. Wrung. And it wasn't getting any easier. First of all, his ugly devil-claw, then whatever was gnawing at her. She's got a kid, he thought. Or maybe she can't have kids. Maybe a crippled mother needing constant care. Time spent in a mental ward. Anything shaping shame, anything she'd think he could hold against her. He couldn't imagine anything unforgivable, but he feared her fear.

He tipped up the frypan in the sink to drain. Dane dried his hands and threw the towel, collapsed into a chair. What next? He wondered how he would see Janine with her unnamed burden—would he recognize her, would he be so accepting then? Lord, he hadn't really kissed her yet, crazy with wanting. Then the question whether their bodies would fit together at all, or fumble and stall in uncertainty. Only more highs and lows, more troubles and excitement ahead and, quite possibly, the outcome of landing on his ass in a big, sore heap. Why couldn't he be flat out giddy and excited, optimistic; did that joy ever come clean and sure, or only in TV movies, in popular songs?

He exhaled, laced his fingers over his knee, orphan three in between the four good fingers, the lone thumb latched. They fit together perfectly. No one would ever guess anything amiss. The country station kicked into a new song. Damn it, he thought, she should know he had it in him to see her whole; and his shoulders eased a little.

The song playing was one he liked, knew well enough to sing in the shower. One of the happy ones. He got up and rummaged around for a clean sheet of paper and a pen. Then he turned off the radio and sat at the Formica table. With his wayward left hand, he laboriously copied in print letters, as neatly as he could, lyrics to the song he knew by heart, every repetition of the chorus in full. At the bottom he wrote, "I'm bad with words but what this song says is exactly the way I feel about you." Signed his name. The song had the word "love" in it. He looked at it a good while, his own painstaking print, the words; then got up and put it in the drawer where he kept the lease and other important papers. He sighed and felt like singing, and like breaking something.

LIVES OF MAPMAKERS

The Map: a statement of the known and the conjectured. A chart, a blueprint. A vision, a meeting of art and science. The map itself goes nowhere; it merely suggests the voyage.

How should we read the map? Embrace the whole, look at contours, then examine the lovingly rendered details? Scan from left to right, top to bottom? Focus on bearings and latitudes, or admire pictorial flourish? Each part illuminates the whole, and vice versa. The master who made it envisioned all these, and many other ways of viewing.

The mapmaker's conundrum: the sphere of the Earth is a thing half-known. He relies on the tales and charts of adventurers to fill the parchment's empty borders with newfound lands, new seas, unseen wonders of Creation. Out on these vast nameless oceans, flat charts don't account for the curve of the globe, and sailors slowly stray. So how is the explorer to go forth and return, without a map?

Oceans ripple like silken fabric far below de Costa; islands appear as tailor's chalk and pincushions, work in progress, a map slowly becoming familiar: the Chinese coast, the Japanese islands, the once mythic Orient a mere jet ride away. He knows Karasuma is old. De Costa has been to Kyoto before to see him. But that was when they were younger, when he thought money would suffice.

Yes, there are other extant Mercator maps; plates from the Europe series, the Atlas in its Hondius editions. A mere professor can afford one of those. But it's Mercator's World Map of 1569, that splendid vision, which de Costa has set his heart on. The World! A Western Hemisphere to the Earth, a newly encountered East, continents modestly revealing their now-familiar shapes. Its revolutionary mathematical projection, the judicious standard against which later maps are judged. Only four copies left in the world, and only one that de Costa has a prayer of getting, the one in private hands—Karasuma's.

De Costa, an Argentine, long ago made his mark on the world, forged an industrial and mercantile empire. His conquests are memorialized in balance sheets and stockholder reports, the *Financial Times.* He keeps several homes—the fine horses at his ranch in Argentina, while his daughters prefer the gaudy energy of Miami. All this, but de Costa doesn't have the map. It took his people six years to track down this fourth copy—its disappearance from the Netherlands, through the centuries and rumors, and finally, to Japan.

On the plane, he flips through an auction catalog, but de Costa hears of treasures long before such things are printed. He has no interest in artifacts of the journey, so he thumbs past pages listing Stanley's desk, Scott's discarded snowshoes. It's maps that intrigue him, coastlines and rivers captured from obscurity. Man is born a hunter, he often tells his wife; he is born to race the wind on horseback, to dig for lost treasures. Luckily for her, he says, he is not a sailor in love with the sea, has no wish to climb Everest. De Costa loves his horses. He loves his art, in the usual way. But he will never rest until Karasuma gives him the vital map. De Costa is not quite as old as Karasuma yet he hears time's tread, and he fears that money won't suffice.

The Great Mapmaker Gerhard Mercator. Poor fellow, he goes down in history, like so many others, with his name transposed to stultifying Latin (although it does have a slightly imperial ring to it, that imperious OR ending), merely the translation of his suitable and honest name: Kremer, merchant. Born anno domini 1512 to German parents in Rupelmonde, Flanders, on the river Schelde (51 degrees 08' north, 4 degrees 17' east, by modern reckoning), close enough to great cities that get news, Köln and Düsseldorf to the east, Antwerp to the north. He is born into an inquisitive and uncertain age, into a poor family. He watches the river's busy trade, the hopes of a rising merchant class that builds fortunes on wool and butter, and soon, Indonesian spices, and North American furs, and what else?

You'll find him busy at his desk, as most visitors do, studious fellow, fussing with his notations. But don't expect an ordinary cartographer, a mere scribe, dear heavens, no; this is an adventure tale, and he needs a worthy introduction.

Mercator (that is, Kremer) first made his mark at Louvain's University, a hot spot of its time, when halls still echoed with the voice of mighty Erasmus. He was a diligent scholar, yet he, too, laments the cost of beer between composing drinking songs in Latin, joins debates on that locally published bestseller, More's *Utopia.* A quiet fellow with a long face, he is an unusual geographer for his day—a wily mathematician, an astronomer, investigator. He has dirtied his hands as a skilled engraver, surveyor, builder of instruments. He married a bright-eyed, sensible girl and set up house, labors dutifully. Who came knocking on his door and said, my good man, it's time to map the world? How did such an idea possess him?

Perhaps vivid tales of explorers sparked an impressionable young mind—even *Utopia* mentions brave Captain Vespucci. However it comes, the obsession for mapping has Kremer by the throat. After some lucky breaks, some powerful mentors, Kremer began to establish his name—rather, the Mercator name—with his own maps, a globe. The printing press, the copper plate, the annual book fair—he has the right genius at the right time—when Europe clamors for the latest discoveries, hungers to see its universe on the page.

Skip a heartbeat.

The burgeoning career was almost clipped—that fearful business with the arrest, the tentacles of the Inquisition, a prison stay that still feeds nightmares. His wife was wise to urge the move east to Duisburg on the Rhine, near the Duke's court. Once there, his work has blossomed; he almost forgets the scars of his imprisonment. He is happy in his study with windows of fine glass that open on his new garden. Since 1554, when his map of Europe in fifteen panels earned international acclaim, the correspondence floods in from Spain, Portugal, England.

The great man is a good neighbor, a benignly negligent father, a tinkerer; he observes the flight of geese, stakes his tender saplings just so. Tolerably kind to his wife, who keeps him in hot pea soup and rye bread through the long, dank winter afternoons when cold makes fingers cramp around his stylus, brings him a shot of nice gin or brandy in the evening, and coals in the brass foot-warmer to tuck under the featherbeds, since her own feet are so chill and comfortless. He has no wish to knock God from His heaven in seeking a new cosmology, no, not Kremer; in these times, best to be quiet on matters of faith. Martin Luther has things in an uproar, and the wars of religion grow more bloody . . . it's plain to see why any fool with a caravel or galleon escapes by sailing, sailing for all he is worth, into the eye of unseen dangers in search of virgin lands, journeying on faith.

No, Kremer thinks, fondly eyeing the plump tree-buds out the window, he will stay at home and stick with cosmo*graphy*, world-writing. The world is still a thing half-known, its corners as black as those of his study, unreached by the lamp's yellow light on a spring evening. Tonight, the calculations torment him, wriggling like eels. Kremer dislikes the sour lacuna of the unknown; he might have been an explorer, but he dislikes the miseries of travel—queasy carriage rides and flea-ridden beds. Alas, he has no sea-legs, has never even crossed "the Sleeve" between Normandy and England. Instead, he reconciles the words of other travelers, noting latitudes and bearings in cramped notation. He frets over the safety of many ships, not just one.

He inhabits a world that genially waits for hearty sea-captains to possess its lands and oceans merely by naming them, by sketching their features on a scrap of sheepskin and planting a flag amid the barnacled rocks. And Kremer (or Mercator) scouts out the news, eats his pork (the New World potatoes haven't reached the north), buys his wife a new pair of crewel-worked slippers; he calmly makes his calculations. He inks letters to Dieppe and Lisbon, seeking more details for engravings. He yearns to move beyond fairy-tale renderings of the discoveries, to something more true. In his dim study, the mapmaker creates worlds.

The map: Why does it inspire such passion? His lush shading of the coasts, tiny topography of molehill mountains, breathtaking inset of the conjectured Arctic! It is Mercator who gives hope of a north or south passage to Europeans yearning for a generous Orient. It was he who found the error in the accepted length of the Mediterranean, corrected the contours of Great Britain. The man was a genius at posing the overlooked question. This brave invention, this one map, changes everything.

Wild men, these restless seekers of discoveries. Some ponder the heavens and labor over calculations, relocate the sun in its cosmos. Others voyage forth, stalwart men known by rough palms and brown necks, the flicker in the eye, captains cagey about trade winds. Some stay at home, quill in hand, patient.

You who would understand the map must know it reveals a war story, a love story, a soap opera. Nothing is what it seems. The plot is one of search and desire, a quest to obtain a certain vision of the world. A tale of hungers, a mad race: for souls, for land, for fame and riches. The vector that shapes the plot is the explorer's special gift, expectation. All journeys begin with faith, the search for an expected end—a tyrannical notion that sends so many astray, sure they have found the Spice Islands when they've reached unimagined western seas, instead. For complications, there are doldrums and reefs, partial and faulty charts, coldhearted storms. The farther from home, the less book-learning carries—Latin and algebraic formulae don't combat the scurvy or bind tattered shoes. Trust and determination alone (and some Native kindness, bark-sure, portage-wise, and unthanked) sustain voyagers in the face of altered hopes and unsurmised endings.

The news that renders coastlines on parchment comes from explorers. Yet how is the explorer to read his way and to return, without a map?

The Great Khan, resplendent in his palace, was curious about the ratty-tatty Venetians with their fulsome luggage who came staggering through the late thirteenth century. What a strange entourage from the west! So soiled and weary were those rough-clad emissaries. Such barbaric beards and round, surprised eyes at the sight of the Mongol monarch. Bad manners, dingy clothes. Yet young Marco Polo proved an able storyteller. Who knows what he invented of his fetid island city-state to impress the king? He made it out to be a nation, a continent: a land of plenty, free of plague and famine, where everyone wears such soft woolens, bears bright metals. Young Polo entranced the Asian lords, spinning European tapestries through interpreters. Perhaps he brought Venetian glass beads and trinkets, too.

The Khan told his own stories. The Huns, his ancient forbears, were adventurers. Centuries before, Attila's hordes had hurtled across the steppes and into Europe's grubby cities on their small, magnificent horses, driving Franks and Vandals and Visigoths west before them. Seating his guests for tea, the king told how Chinese rulers had sent their own explorers to Java, India, ambassadors armed with split bamboo, brushes and black cakes of ink to record their travels. He exalted the courage of his own warriors, their conquests, and kept to himself their failures. Thus it continued, trading tales of strange lands through many nights of feasting.

And Polo returned to Venice, with his souvenirs and noodles, and published his *Travels*, his version. Three centuries later, in 1584—as an elderly Mercator engraved his latest book—a Portuguese monk, Fra Matteo Ricci, compiled a world map using Chinese characters and printed it from woodblocks in Nankin. But whose version is this? An unrecognizable world with two half-spheres. Ancient Chinese maps fixed China as the center, while other nations bobbed as islands in an all-surrounding sea. But with the monk's rendering, mighty China is pushed to the edge, the periphery, of a world centered elsewhere. Without a single lance or cannon. With ink.

At twelve hours's difference from Buenos Aires, Japan is a clean hemisphere away. De Costa tries to sleep for a few restless hours in the over-firm hotel bed, but he feels his travels weigh within his face. He reviews his opening moves as he dresses.

Karasuma's lieutenant, a broad-shouldered young man, seats de Costa in a conference room with antique porcelains on display—in the open, as if they weren't priceless. De Costa can guess that much, though he doesn't know Ming from Tang. Maps form the only overlap in the collections of the two men. He tugs the sleeve of his custom-tailored linen suit. The air conditioning is almost too cool—de Costa likes warm climates, the sun on his face. Outside, below the windows, fruit trees swell with pale pink buds. The young man returns and asks de Costa to follow.

Karasuma bows, and so does de Costa. Their complexions are similar: ebony eyes, sallow skin. Their flesh is similarly loose at the jaw. But de Costa carries bulk, and Karasuma has receded even in the years since their last meeting; his spine relents ever so slightly, but his eyes are still stony. Not unkind, Karasuma, ever polite—but firm. De Costa's eyes hide in pouches, droopy folds.

They trade token gifts. The visitor already knows what his host will drink, and he requests scotch also. The two men, one in his seventies, one in his late fifties, make polite chit-chat, a part of the ritual de Costa has come to enjoy. In a common language, they inquire after the health of each other's families, each person by name, cluck over the unpleasant accents and loud familiarity of their children's American friends. They discuss shipping and steel, industries in which neither of them invest. Karasuma's assistant leads them to a private dining room, and only after they have daubed hands with steamed towels and eaten well does the matter surface.

"I am most curious," says Karasuma in his impeccable Oxford English, "as to why you think my answer will have changed."

"Ah," says de Costa, "perhaps it's the question that has changed?"

Karasuma barely, just barely, smiles. "I do not think so," he says, "but I will listen."

De Costa appears languid and relaxed in his movements, but a little navy-blue vein pulses below his ear. "Fair enough," he says. "You know I want the Mercator 1569 World Map. There are many wonders in the world; perhaps there is one that has eluded your grasp, one you cannot stop wanting, and I may be of service. Name it, and I will get it. And trade for the Mercator."

Karasuma puts down his drink. "What makes you think that there is anything, anything at all that I still want?"

"Because," says the visitor, "we are both collectors. That desire is in our blood."

"You are in the East, my friend. Here, desire is a private thing. My collection is my secret, one you took great pains to discover. I do not share it with the world." Karasuma says this gravely, but de Costa detects a twinkle in his eye.

"I have made some inquiries," de Costa begins. He makes his proposals: a certain Majorcan portolan map; a certain rare Dutch postage stamp. As he expected, Karasuma seems indifferent. It is part of the chase. As expected, de Costa leaves empty-handed.

What is a continent or coastline? An idea, a belief. An assertion of order. Such things cannot be seen by human eye—no more than one man can see Frankfurt-am-Main from Düsseldorf. Only when man alights on moon can whole lands be seen, in darling miniature. A continent, its coast, is a series of forays, pieces to be assembled. A map is a mosaic, patchwork of visions, a story. An agreement between hand and eye, a sequence of tiny nib-strokes on vellum.

A Note About God and Cosmography

Oh, the woes of upstart Christianity. Its God sat resplendent, central, in medieval European maps as He was in their cosmos, the Holy Land the center of Creation, until, until . . . Moors drove the Crusaders from Palestine, Christians turned their wrath upon the scapegoat Jews. Until Claudius Ptolemy, that pesky, long-dead Alexandrian, upended Christian cosmography when his writings were recovered—then even maps turned their backs on Jerusalem. By 1400, mapmakers showed Ptolemy's rectangular shoe-box of Eurasia wrapping well around the globe, Africa a lost sock dangling below.

Then geography and geometry rule; God becomes a monarch without a country.

Vigilance against heresy is needed when the Cosmos itself is in flux.

To the fixed eye, we almost don't appear to move; the bow cleaves calm seas, sails taut and silent; land stays to starboard, greenly, evenly. Will we ever get there? Is "getting" the point? Not to me. In fact, *not* getting is more to the point; a long run sailing up and down the Sound. Lean, and look ahead, see that feathering surface? The necessary skill—reading the wind's footprints, how the tell-tales whip from the stays. In a smaller boat, I'd make her heel up, and we'd ride high on the gunwale for ballast. Up then down, I'd tweak the tiller, Up Down, like a bronco, and you'd squeal and yell. Ready? Prepare to come about. No, no, a destination doesn't concern me. I just like going.

1492

The watershed year. That sly fellow Behaim in Nuremburg unveils the first globe of the Earth, not the heavens. A novel presentation of an oft-discussed idea, a shocking display—since Portugal and Castile treat maps as state secrets in the race for new lands. The year when the Jews are expelled from Spain, questing for safe haven yet again. That same year, a rough-hewn mariner named Cristobal Colón plants Spanish colors on a green island, sure that he has found the Indies. That misnomer will stick for centuries, even as the future Admiral Colón seeks the Great Kahn's palace on Cuba, estimates the Ganges River near Mexico.

The Taino are not so happy, on their island that they do not call Watling or San Salvador. Discovery, what discovery? We were never lost . . . .

Henceforth, those lands will lose their people once the captain's brother, Bartholomeo Colón, or *Columbus* in the Latinate, makes the maps which guide adventurers there. Pale-faced voyagers kidnap the New World's first slaves; a new trail of blood begins. Don't look for the Taino. You will not hear from them again.

By the century's turn, latitudes have been marked on a map, the secrets are published, and sea-captains become heroes. Da Gama heads south, Cabot and the Corteréal brothers sail north and west, Covilhão seeks India via the Red Sea, and never fear for Amerigo Vespucci. He'll turn up eventually and he'll be right as rain. No cognates of his name linger in modern Italian dictionaries. In French, *amer* means bitter, or (less commonly and nautically) a landmark, a recognizable feature visible from sea. Explorers learn how bitter a landmark can be: the long-desired promontory obstructed by a swamp of blade-sharp saw palmetto; wind-stunted oaks and impassable beach-rose on a coastal prominence; southern jungle, thick with liana vines and parrots; but nowhere, nowhere, nowhere, the sought-for bustling harbors, the palaces of the Khans, silk-merchants with their jewel-bright ells, the fine herds of the Asian horsemen, and all the golden riches of Cathay.

Beyond the sideyard with its sundial and jonquils, behind tiny panes of thin, costly glass, there lurks a spy. Danger scents his very shoes. Inside sits a man who keeps secrets from his wife, lies about business trips to see his patron, a man who steals out the back gate at night with the duplicity of an adulterer.

Mercator follows his Flemish guide up the stairs of a new brick warehouse on a harbor pier. A rank smell of low tide pursues him. Windows admit late afternoon sun to the small counting room on the second floor, and a dark man materializes from behind the door—the informant, who has come here to Rotterdam by ship. The first man, Kniep, interprets as the Majorcan produces a folded parchment from inside his doublet. Mercator works quickly—he does not know how this copy has been smuggled, nor its origin. All three are wary, quiet. To reveal such finds is treason, death.

The rudely inked map seems to show a sweep of the northeast coast of that grand new continent Mercator has called North America, following Waldseemüller's lead. Someone has explored this thrust of coastline in secret—the Portuguese, Mercator guesses from the notation. The mapmaker recognizes the shape of Terre Corterealis there above the Sinus St. Laurentii. He quizzes the nervous Majorcan through the translator, pointing. "What can you tell me of this river? To which inlet do these figures apply?"

The man is brown as a sailor, shows a sailor's knowledge as he explains the newly detailed gulf—its river mouths, fierce currents, great slabs of ice. The men jump as a door bangs somewhere below; they wait in silence, wait, and breathe once more.

"How do the tides run here?" Mercator asks. His eyes shine like flints. "The prevailing winds? At full sail, how long to round this point?"

The man gestures, Mercator nods, jots notations, asks about the movements of seals and seabirds. This source, like so many others, will remain forever secret. He will compare it to Fine's 1531 map, consult with his colleague Ortelius. The Majorcan grows more edgy as the questions drag on; though he's obviously weathered great trials and his hands are hard as oak, a sweat breaks out on his face, neck. When he's finally released from the interrogation, he asks to be paid in the coin of the Lowlands and hurries out alone, sliding into the cold shadows of ships that crowd the pier.

Even the master feels a rivulet of fear at these moments. Mercator finishes his notes and follows his guide silently down the steep stairs, but a trick of light in the dark stairwell, that close space—and for an instant he's back in a cold prison. He grips at the wall.

It's a primal panic that surfaces: the dreadful surge he felt at the sound of footfalls in the dark beyond his prison cell. For long months, he lived in fear among creeping vermin and cold; no maps, no family, no garden. The Church dislikes change and challenge. The Inquisitors queried him daily about his associates, his secretive journeys, probing his quiet Protestantism for imagined heresies. He still has scars from torture by a zealous cleric attempting to force confessions. Even his Court connections didn't help; only Mercator's brave defenders at the university won his freedom. On the narrow stair, he gasps for air, fights a panic born of memory and shadows.

Surely—he tells himself—probably he's protected now

by his appointment as court cosmographer to the Duke of Cleves. Yet still these furtive meetings hold danger; more perils than shipwreck attend great discoveries. But there's no help for it. He breathes deeply of the harbor smell to try to focus his mind. Mercator glances behind him, tucking the precious scrap close to his heart, and plunges down, into the twilight.

At this point, the reader may grow anxious for a landmark, some progress . . .

Whether man or colt, the progress is the thing; the vessel's advance, even by tacking back and forth into a head wind. Progress is evidenced by a change in position of the landmark relative to the traveler, a shift of perspective. Landmarks are always tall: Balboa's peak, and Zebulon Pike's. Or they are low: waterways, straits, estuaries, a fluid trail leading to the Great Something, a flood finding its own shape.

The Huns, the Huns, the Huns. Westward they fly on their sharp-shinned mounts; myths spawn before them, centaur and pegasus, man-steeds, fierce. Pawing and snorting, a tattoo of hoofbeats. Centuries gallop. Later, Mohammedans drive into Europe on agile Arabian horses. Their forays will draw the wrath of Crusaders back upon Eastern empires—those long holy wars begin. But first, hot blood of the Orient's horses will liven the stock of the knights' heavy mounts. Thick chests, strong haunches, fierce hearts. Sturdy gray and brown mares, restive stallions, dust-heaving whirlwinds: to east and west, the victory goes to horsemen.

Centuries later, fine Andalusian chargers quiver and snort, their fire subdued by the long Atlantic crossing. Brown eyes blink, sun-blinded after weeks in the ship's dark hold. The place smells wrong; they balk.

An instant that alters two civilizations.

Spaniards ply the lash. Then those first-ever hoofprints labor the Mexican shore: panicked, slurred, deep.

De Costa departs Japan, momentarily frustrated. He knows a commander must stomach small setbacks. Yet these trips are always exhilarating, too. Only Karasuma understands, though he doesn't use terms like "passion." De Costa smiles; they are like two men reminiscing on an old flame. On the plane, he plots his course toward the map that has become his future. This is the map that changes everything: the world is never seen the same way again. An artistic triumph; a scientific landmark! No more lands to conquer, de Costa muses—but their images, the moment of their conception in one mind, that genius can be acquired. The genius that unfurled the globe on the page in such splendor. He reclines his seat, looks forward to the soothing ritual of currying his favorite horse Vendaval, sharing dinner with his wife.

When it comes to the map, his wife says he's crazy, and she's right. It is a love, a passion, the kind that makes him feel young. But it bears the weight of centuries.

His wife is not his greatest love, though she does not know this. Those incendiary laurels will always belong to another, chestnut-haired, stormy-eyed. Neruda's love sonnets, certain constellations in the sky, will always belong to her. De Costa recognizes this for what it is: a young man's love, first passion. His marriage is built on deep love: banked coals, the love that's possible after loss. Love that is precious because it reckons its costs.

And it is the costs that make him love the map. This map is a flag on a warship and the first Greek column. The risks it takes, the costs to its master, de Costa can guess. Yet still he will speak, this Mercator; he wills to shape this world with exactitude. De Costa thinks, the struggles of the pathmakers are always the same.

As the moon rises slowly in the evening sky, Karasuma punches the phone, calls in his eldest son. He can see the blossoms in the gardens below, old trees flush with fresh petals. Osamu waits politely for his father's nod to sit; the elder Karasuma takes an armchair opposite. His eyes shine.

"The Argentine was here again," he says, "about the Mercator map."

"What did he offer you this time?"

Karasuma flutters his hand in a motion that implies—go away. "He thinks there is something I will trade for it." He asks his son to get him a drink of water. His son runs the company now, politely soliciting his father's advice.

The son pours from an antique porcelain pitcher, offers the cup to his father on a small tray. "And you let him think that?"

"Of course." He smiles. "We are almost friends over the love of this map. Every few years he comes to see me, every time he makes a new offer. He expects to find the one thing I cannot resist."

"If there is something, surely this is the man to get it. He wants that map very badly," the son laughs lightly. "You are the one to set the price, any price."

"There is always a price," muses Karasuma, and takes a sip of water.

A man stands at a window, rubbing at his wrist. Outside, the fragile greens of spring are unfurling. He thinks of ships that rock like horses with a merchant's wager in the hold. His mind wanders: a gift for his wife, a blank space waiting on the wall, the fortunes of a child continuing a father's legacy. In his complicated wrist he feels the cost of what must be told, the force of words engraved in type. A matter of interpretation. He ponders his place in the hemisphere. He wishes for more fruit trees in the yard: apple, cherry. A male, he doesn't worry about the act or cost of possession.

What's in a name? Names have power. A man's name reveals the blessing of a godfather, an invocation of a saint. It tells of a trade, a landmark, a trait: Marsh, Smith, Shortsleeve; de Rivera, Charpentier, Kremer—Merchant. In the Age of Discovery, men do not own their names and new lands live anonymously. European explorers possess lands by affixing Latin names, names that refer to their homes, their monarchs, the familiar . . . except the alluring *Terra Incognita*, the unknown land. Lands are described as fertilely female, desiring to be possessed, requesting names with feminine-voweled endings.

Other explorers look inward: in anatomy, bones are Latin-named for function or shape—*blade*, *shaft*, *turning*—two wrist bones named "boat-like" and "crescent." Secretive dissection is all the rage, and laying bare the mysteries, Leonardo Da Vinci inks from cadavers. Florentine painters explore the principle of perspective and it slowly travels north. Perspective demands a vision and a viewer, implies a single creator; a version seen yet never absolute. Possession, morphology, exactitude, function, but where's beauty? Today I'll inscribe small mountains, hatch borders, ink in round italics. Today I think o's, n's and k's sound lovely and I'll keep all those names: *Okeefenokee, Monongahela, Bokhara, Kyoto, Nicobar, Samarkand, Orinoco, Orinoco, Orinoco.*

Poor Gerhard Mercator. His blessing and his curse, to be born to the "Renaissance," though of course, no one calls it that at the time. At the moment, the curse is directed to his quill, which has snapped and sent a blot of ink the shape of Sardinia onto his calculations. The globe plays havoc with a map's single plane. He is working on a better system of projection that shows constant bearings—a new way of looking at the page. The possibilities leave him breathless, but it is slow work. He throws the offending feather to the floor and plucks another from the tray.

Cartography is a troublesome business, he mutters, not for the timid. A map had always been a rare thing: a tool for sailors, functional as a marlinspike, or a title-deed for princes, guarded on pain of death. The printing press changed all that. But now there is so much news, and problems of calculation, sources that disagree. The nib scratches away. One degree of the earth's orb, how shall that be measured in nautical miles? Of what span is *degree*?

Mercator reviews notes penned in his economical hand, worries a thumb into his beard. He has already lived to the half-century, one life's span—has buried his eldest son—yet there is never enough time. So much has been revealed since his map of '38 with those astounding twinned continents to the west. Now, freshly printed accounts provide descriptions of New France, and a newly charted island of Japan; travels up the Amazona and Orinoco rivers, and to the iceberg-laden seas above Finland. Positions of new discoveries migrate wildly, depending on each explorer's royal patron. It seems every sea-captain is an author, he tells the inkpot: Columbus and Vespucci as disciples of Polo, spinning yarns, staking claims. News from cartographers in Normandy, Texeira's prolific chartings from the Moluccas (does he never rest?). He blinks; the genius's eyes tire in the poor light. How is one to keep up, after all, sitting in one's study in Duisburg? Just too much information, the fast pace of technology, in this modern sixteenth century.

His grandchildren burst in, clamoring for "a trip to the fair, Best-Papa, and sweet-meats, Gretchen says there are jugglers, please?"

Mercator steadies the inkpot, tells them to hush. "Mapmaking isn't some work of fancy," he chides. These maps establish the shape of the world! It's his pen-stroke, the burin on copper plate, that fixes the shifting shape of knowledge. Once named, shaped, printed, such versions take on the flesh of fact. He acutely feels the burden of lives of brothers on the seas, dependent on his charts to avoid the equatorial doldrums, to provision themselves accurately—a few degrees off, and weeks weaken sailcloth, men go hungry . . .

He stops his lecture at the children's somber faces, sends them bounding off with coppers. They can't understand his passion. His new wool stockings itch. Will his children, grandchildren, set foot on those foreign archipelagos? Whose imagination will fill those blank spaces?

Mercator rubs the callus on his finger where the burin rests. His new projection format accounts for the curve of the Earth; it will greatly help navigators, but the mathematics take time. His eyes trouble him, yet he is driven to late, lamp-lit nights. The latest batch of quills is inferior, brittle, the nibs he cuts snap right off, and the little pear and apple trees in the garden, in this harsh spring, they're not doing well at all.

The sea-captain's dilemma: the captain sails to find the far, conjectured shore and fix it as fact; he must keep the ship in wind and on bearing, fill his hold, reach home and tell his stories to the king and his mapmaker. He sails with high hopes and expectations of gain. Yet what if he eddies endlessly in a New World Charybdis, snaps masts in some Western sirocco, just keeps sailing without sight of land?

At last, the brave captain Amerigo Vespucci returns. It is quite an era, 1482-1502. As the ancients proposed, the world proves a sphere indeed—its other half encountered by sailors like him, like Dias and da Gama, helming creaking crescent-like ships, square-rigged, barque-rigged, agile caravels lateen-rigged with triangle sails borrowed from feluccas. Captain Vespucci returns in 1501, haunted by the fragrant, secretive lands he's seen, all promise and impervious green—east coast of Cabral's great Southern Continent. The vision burns him like a brand: a haughty virgin land withholding her dower: no spices, no silks, no gold. Denied the mythic passage west to a generous Orient, he returns as merely a captain whose voyages fire the imagination, home with tales to tell and mappings to make. The bitter taste lingers in his mouth, but something else will live on.

Cosmographiae Introductio: a tale told in coasts and compass roses. Far north of Amerigo's sunny home, in a Rhineland of sweet, pale grapes and hunting woods, the mapmaker Martin Waldseemüller is at work. In 1507, he parts company with old Ptolemy to embrace the captain's discoveries with his world maps, his *Cosmographiae*—wood-block print, twelve sheets. And there it is in print, the Fact unseen by the ancients—*terre nove*, New Land, not an elbow of Asia as Vespucci first suspected, gliding past its lush, green-sloped shoulders. The name Amerigo Vespucci enters history as the name this cosmographer gives to a vast land interrupting a western sea—*America*. The great Mercator is born in the very year the captain goes to meet his Maker, and in 1538 Mercator is the first to use the name to designate *two* new bodies, half-curled lovers blocking the way west: North America and South America, forever linking hands but drawn apart.

Names that endure.

Yes, by 1538, all manner of things have been discovered and destroyed. The west coast of the Cabral's continent has been mapped, Cortés has crushed the Aztec empire, de Elcaño has finished ill-fated Magellan's circumnavigation, Cartier has claimed the St. Lawrence estuary. By then, California has been charted, and it is clear, too clear, that we're not in Asia anymore; Oceanus Pacificus dashes that dream. Those new bodies bar the westward voyage to the Indies, for now.

Amerigo, these blessed bodies with their stony backbones, they have their place. *America.* Centuries later, your name has the weight of myth, of promise and impossibility, all around the charted world. It is the known and the unknown, the North-South-Central, the United States of. *America*, bitter and rich, a landmark; a Latinized name with hard rocky consonants and a feminine ending, like every other.

"The price," muses Karasuma. "The cost, the coast: did you know that is the meaning of his name, de Costa? Interesting, isn't it? It pays to know one's opponent. Though he is not my opponent, cannot be, while I hold the map." He sighs, an old man, resisting his fatigue. "De Costa is not looking for the map. He is looking for himself."

"Oh, really?" Osamu looks indulgently at his father, until corrected by a stern expression.

"Learn from me, Harvard boy. I'm your elder yet." His eyes search the teak-paneled office, the quartz moon rising, the gnarled cherry trees below. It was hard for him, permitting Osamu to go the United States, even though he's a reasonable man, even though Kyoto was spared. Even though a blinding detonation showed the world is no longer big enough for such enmity. He sighs. His son is a citizen of the world in the way all young people now are. "I am on speaking terms with my ancestors. I live in their land, I speak their speech. De Costa, he suffers the pains of the displaced. Something haunts him." He takes a sip of water. "I have often wondered . . . Juan de la Cosa, the navigator of Columbus. He left one hand-drawn map—I saw it years ago in Madrid—at any rate, their names are very similar. Perhaps de Costa is related to this man?"

"So . . . you think he's searching for an ancestor?"

"Or perhaps he simply loves this map. Merely my amusing idea, for what it's worth." Karasuma looks out the window at the cobalt sky. "When a man reaches a certain age, he realizes there are no new territories, were never any—only those unseen by his eyes. Only possessions that change hands. We must hold our treasures lightly."

The son studies his father's face. "Perhaps there is a Ming porcelain he could get for you—he might make a deal with a museum for a Ming piece, trade the Ming to you for the Mercator. Or would you sell to him?"

Through the window, the old man sees cherry blossoms glow like porcelain in the deepening darkness. He has a secret, hides a smile. It has all been decided—in a codicil to his will. His children will not mind; to them, the map is valued only for its rarity, an item to be inventoried. To their father, it means much more; the map must be earned through devotion, journeys, sacrifice. A certain order must be maintained among men of stature; the word he thinks of is close to "duty" and "care." De Costa has the heart of a sea captain, the heart of a mapmaker. They understand each other. Karasuma rises slowly, to avoid succumbing to the stiffness in his knees. "I would sell to him before any other. But I won't. I would not do that to a friend."

At times, the wrist begins to ache. So much tension on the mainsheet, so much pressure on the quill, so much typing. It is a delicate thing, the wrist: anatomical atlases show small bones neatly stacked, sturdy contours forming tiny passages, bones that want their own names back. Two tendons thread the narrow tunnel and, inflamed, they complain often. *We are overworked with explaining!* they whine; *can't you find your own way?* No hand, no map; no gesture, no pointing at the landmark to show, there, there! If we were left with mute hands, with merely the conqueror's Latin words, we'd never get anywhere. They'd swell in our mouths, bloat in all the narrow straits, and we'd never be able to tell the wonders we'd seen.

Gerhard Kremer, let your heavy eyelids fall. The great work is almost done—only the final flourishes to the borders, some last detail to the magnificent oceans. Your new method of projecting all those lands changes their shapes. There is the delicate isthmus claimed by Balboa, there the northern gulf supplied by the Majorcan—a region that will not be charted so accurately again for three centuries. God's Creation is magnificent in your eyes, and you spend decades conveying it through your hand.

Dozing in your study as the light wanes, huddled near the tile stove, even dreams can't tell you how your world will change. The center has shifted so many times across the centuries, borders have been drawn and redrawn across the patch of Europe you call home. It must be a comfort in your old age that your sons have shown an interest; Rumold is a fine engraver, his map of the Hemispheres will be a classic. And when you sleep the long sleep in 1594, he will see your last great work done, the completed Atlas of the World, even as daring Galileo designs his telescope, organizes planets; as Shakespeare unveils bawdy, crowd-pleasing comedies at the Globe. Your name, like theirs, will live on.

You stir and sigh in the fading light. Perhaps you dream of worlds you'll never see, of lofty mountains and natural harbors; trumpet-shaped blossoms big as your hand; the soft, red "gold-apples" the Florentines describe. In the new Hemi-Sphere, soon surveyors will carve states and nations along straight-ruled latitudes, ignoring rivers, swamps, mountains: For the first time, the mapmakers shape the nation, instead of merely recording its borders.

Here, at the dawn of the second millennium, they still bake that tough-crusted rye in Paderborn and jonquils still bloom in March. Scions of the apple trees now flourish in the New World. The Rhine still surges toward the North Sea, but the Lorelei are long gone from the river, my friend. The world whose contours you knew firsthand, of half-timbered villages and brick churches, continues its tempestuous life. Your homelands have been leveled and raised and leveled; have borne duchies, empires, kingdoms, states, borders drawn through fields of barley and those enforced with walls. Brabant, Flanders, Netherlands, Alsace and Lorraine, Prussia, Weimar, Third Reich, France, GDR, Germany.

You'd be pleased that our wars at least have kept the mapmakers busy.

ATLAS

1595

Atlas sive Cosmographicae Meditationes de Fabrica Mundi et Fabricati Figura.
Frontispiece of Mercator's compiled maps of the world:
A muscular man cradles in his arms
the shape of a large globe,
Orbis Terrarum,
The Earth.
This is the first time the name ATLAS is used
to describe a book of maps.
Readers ponder the hunched figure, searching
for myths of origin.
The world a round and groaning weight.

The Mapmaker's Conundrum: The protagonist must have a certain map. It may take him years. But there is only one. The map only—only the map—explains his existence, gives him life. A true map, a map that breaks rules, creates worlds.

Margins.

It has been a strange journey and you dearly want to get to this map. By now, you are tired of Ptolemy, you are getting a little cross at all this palaver, oh yes, I see the droop of your lids. You want a snack. You wonder what to sift, to trust, from all these trinkets, which path to lead you to this famous piece of parchment. It's a struggle, learning how to read a new kind of map.

So many stories bring us to the map; so many maps are merely fairy stories. Even Marco Polo is a myth of his own making, as is his Kublai Khan; as much a fairy story as those old, wishful cosmographies, as lovely and untrue as a child's treasure map. You wonder what's been left out, like the magnetic compass, and the voiceless peoples of the "new" worlds; wonder what the lovely "compass rose" denotes and wonder most, whatever will happen to the mapmaker, and the collector? The common end, of course. Perhaps you should wonder what else lies neglected in the bare margins: greed, violence and betrayals. Pains of the deckhand and his palm burned by hemp. Informers and rivals. Names of women who birthed and nourished captains and cartographers, names of peoples vanquished. What else has been forgotten? That the Aztecs saw Spanish horses as strange deer. That a hundred years before the *Mayflower* reached Cape Cod, Estavão Gomes charted the New England coast, a hemstitched line of points and inlets inscribed in ink. Wonder, was it his men, Cabot's, Cartier's, who left the gift of pox there while on shore leave, a gift to those Pilgrims of abandoned cornfields, a thinly peopled coast? Wonder that your grandparents didn't see a space-made photo of the whole and turning Earth until they were gray and claimed they wanted nothing. Whose version is this, anyway?

The explorer braves great uncertainty, needs fierce imagination, to see such vast continuities. The obsessions of such men fuel armies, find stars, conquer rulers, defeat diseases, turn swamps into wheatfields. Don't you care about the first time the term "Atlas" was used? About the beauty of names for rivers, ships, winds? You may think what is known now was always, that it bore the same names; that is your myth.

This map contains all those stories, names, and houses all those hiding and forgotten. An enabling distortion, one that poses curved lines as straight and stretches shapes of coasts at their far edges—a world mathematically true and never to be seen by the eye.

Perhaps that is too much to ask. I, de Costa, I am a collector. I love the 1569 Mercator with all the passion of explorers for the Magic Isle, the zeal of a captain for his ship. I love its beautiful, blocky contours of South America, more like a green bell pepper than a tapered chile. Accurate Africa. Broad-shouldered North America, overlong; mythical isle of Frisland, slanted Greenland. I love the curling italic type, his innovation, which gives such distinctive, graceful appeal. The care, the care. And not the least, his brilliant innovation, the "waxing latitudes": a trapezoidal projection of those now-familiar continents that runs true at the Equator, broadens at the poles. Boon to navigators, it renders longitudinal meridians parallel on a flat map, gives constant bearings. This splendid map debuts the Mercator Projection, the shapes of continents which every schoolchild recognizes today. This map changes the world.

Why do I care? Why does any collector, any lover? The beloved has no flaws; her flaws are singularly and preciously of her, therefore not flaws. I love without reason. I love his ink and downstroke, I love the curl of his serif. The mind behind such diligent, resourceful effort. The Earth has been pinned in its solar system, God in His heavens, the gene within its raveling chromosome. The only thing left is to want: the only thing left to want is my 1569 Mercator.

Desire is like water, it is life. I will go again to Japan. The Mercator: a new way of reading a new world, a moment in the existence of the old. I will go to my map room and sit there, at the sunscreened window overlooking the pampas; then I will pull down the protective shade and in the purpled dimness I will look at the place of honor I have saved for the Mercator 1569 World Map. I will look at it forever. I will look for it forever. What shall I do if I stop wanting The World? The full orb, a world pregnant with hope, a tale always telling.

Women Who Dream of Corn

The women have berry-fingers, light and deft, to pluck, twist stems without bruising flesh. That's what the men want from them, berry-fingers. The men are worn and stained; they want comfort shaped as soft voices, as flesh all dew and suppleness, not as tree-trunks with scarred bark, aching back. Their men, their children, seek refreshment, to be eased and plucked, tended, gently laid in the basket. The women know their place. Tending. Instead, they dream of being straight and tall: pale poplar, oat grass, corn.

Days are long in the fields. The women leave their blood on the ground in splashes and gashes. Their bodies drag over the growing fields, the way Corn Mother's body was dragged. The Mother who told her sons to partition her body and drag it over the soil, drag her flesh to seed the earth, to feed the people. If the women remembered her, they'd know her broken flesh provides, know her as the sheaf laid in the manger; but to them she is only the soft sigh in métis hand-me-downs, the gesture of winnowing. Green rows stretch long. The women scar their hands on stalks and knives and thorns to fill more baskets, buy more sneakers for the children. They talk of going union. They want to buy a trailer. Nikes for the kids and a color TV. They grope down long days of greens and at night they rub salve on their cuts and dream.

The women come from many places. Their names are Luz, Fernanda, Marie-Jeanne, Sonia, Kathie, Olivia, Odette, Yrma, Pearl, Lacey. The sun paints them different shades of brown. Work hews their hands hard. Their labor rules the world into straight edges. Low rows run on toward the highway, on to the stands of ruffling trees that cleave hazy blue Mid-American sky from the fields. The low rows run for miles until an oasis of silvered mesquite. Rows run west until the hills rear up in the Dakotas, or run east to the walls closing in on the San Joaquin valley, from highway to highway. Strawberries, peaches, green beans, cucumbers, tomatoes, move on, move on, south to north, along the migrant routes, hut to hut. Plucking, twisting, gathering, filling, filling.

Strawberry time, and Luz is red-fingered and reeling. Panels of sky keep tilting above her. She teeters right, rights herself, picks again; staggers as she moves down the row of crinkling plants, muttering. "What's that?" Sonia asks, head down. "What are you saying?"

"Nothing," says Luz, but Sonia can hear her, off and on, a sing-song. Focused on her own progress, Sonia doesn't notice how her friend keeps stumbling. The berry scent engulfs them.

Near noon, Luz stands up. She drops her bucket and stands, feet planted wide. "I can't bend no more," she announces. "No. I want to be corn."

The horizon is low and green: squashes, peppers, tomato vines. Things that somehow should feed themselves to a conveyor, shuck and peel themselves, isn't this an automated world? But tender fruit requires tender fingers; every pie-bound berry feels the human touch. The long rows converge before them. All around, their only hills are named Deltoid, Trapezius, the domes of their shoulders, a landscape that travels with them.

So the women want to be tall, straight, and thirsty. They want to hold places in neat rows, hold down the soil veined with clay or sandy-light. Every day they spend bent over, stooped like birches under snow, weight-bowed; after so long, they freeze in arcs so their heads never rise. The women have all day to bend while they pluck and snip, fruit and stem. Each day's rotation of the globe, and gravity pulls them down. Yanks down the hand on the blossom, into the dirt. Hand on the berry, dragged down. Such is the weight of each berry, each head of lettuce. Beans, melons, down.

Luz struggles to hold her balance, as if there were a hard wind.

"Shut up," Sonia calls over her shoulder. "Get moving. Shut up now, you gonna catch hell." She is used to Luz's complaints. The small berries grow so heavy. Luz stretches upwards, her face more like a sunflower, tilted up, as she sways slightly.

The women's shoulders don't want to slide down, ever. Bent back for the orchards, bent down for the greens. At night their spines dream of straightness but retain roundness; they feel unsteady as willow baskets wobbling on the slats. Ghost limbs, their inert arms feel like they hover above the cots, poised and pincered. At night they dream ominous mountains of green peas, threatening hosts of broccoli, sanguine berries. They dream of helming big, shining trucks that peel through the field, doing spin-outs and donuts on the crisp greens, the fertile stalks, grinding them into muddy pulp like day-after-market produce crushed on the street.

Luz knows how corn is. Tall and tough. How the raspy, razor-sharp leaves slice skin. Lasting-tough. She can be in it proudly. "Yes," she calls to all the stooping females, she thinks she is telling a long story, but her lips don't move, and the sun pulses fat above her, within her.

Corn doesn't migrate. Corn doesn't follow the growing season. It stands neat in rows, not folded over, not packed into dark huts or hunched over smoky campfires, doesn't stomp palmetto bugs and pick at ticks and bandage the gashes from the coarse blade. Its roots are shallow. It will give up the soil itself to a high wind rather than bend. Corn will not bend. Through the snows, pale stalks hold their place, chatter and whisper in their muslin tatters. Corn is grass. All it grows, stalk and leaf, is vertical, lined and veined in uprights.

All day, faced away from the sky, the women dream within their muscles of corn. They want to be tall and tasseled, turn their faces to the sun. They yearn to reach up until their palms and elbows fuse in prayer: a spear, a lodge-pole. Something in the bones of their necks remembers the Corn Mother, Barley Mother, Kore, in all her names. Those short bones like flat, stacked kernels of hard gold. As they stretch, the women's black hair will go light and crinkled, float softly, their skins wrinkle in parallel grooves.

Luz sways in the wind no one else feels, arms raised. "I want to be corn," she yells. "I am corn. I'm not bending no more." Her arms are light, hands huge. The fever makes her see clearly. She sees how green she is, how green and fibrous.

Marie-Jeanne hops over a row, pulling a bandana from her pocket. Swipes at sweat streaming down the dark dome of her forehead. "What's up with you now, girl?" Skips another row. "Stop making trouble, now. Hush, now. Hush, now," she says as Luz's voice retreats to a moan. She dances away, keeps her toi-toi rhythm, bouncing.

Sonia advances, laughs at Luz's loco jive. "This new dance, eh?"

"Unhhh, unh," groans Luz, her face panicky, arms jiggering. "I'm all crushed down. Dreamed I was being crushed down. I got to go up."

Marie-Jeanne grabs the woman's arm, lays a moist palm on her forehead. "Lord, you burning up, girl. You feel all right?"

"She's got to go up," Luz whispers. "Woman got to be corn."

Sonia laughs, is ready to give a scolding, till she sees Luz's face, the tears squeezing out of shut eyes, the way she's swaying. They wave for the crew leader. They shake their heads at Luz, her crazy talk.

"Let me be corn," Luz whimpers. "I don't want to fall down. Don't let me fall down," clutching at Sonia's sweaty elbow.

Luz rests in the red truck. She is fevered and chattering for two days, then it breaks and she doesn't remember a thing. She laughs and makes a face at the retelling. But her rantings have infected the others. Her fever speaks for the body, gives shape to strange dreams in their flesh that they all share.

They dream corn is a woman, green and heedless. Its green silken tubules gather, twist and brown once their work is done, soft as the hair of a woman. Blonde silk, dark tangled tassels. Yet they are told woman's role is to be melon-vine: low and creeping, close to the dank earth, shaded, round and gravid. So many want her as round fruit, ripe orange flesh, ovary of slithering pale seeds, sweet and sticky. The women know the melon vine works by indirection, insinuating its tendrils wherever it can, gaining a grasp by stealth, fanning its dark, heavy leaves like an arbor. They have learned viny lessons. Have let themselves be trained, bowing and creeping. They slip in silence toward the next handhold, the next anchor, trying to climb. Their only powers subtlety, a strong grip.

Some days the women wish for shade and fullness, indolence, to be the thing resting and picked. Yet Luz has tapped the dream that runs in the marrow—a craving to be stretched and sturdy. They know fruit only goes soft, pulps and perishes. Corn dries hard and shiny. It rattles in the basket, glitters in the crib, pings into a stony groove and scrapes as stone does its crushing work. Corn endures. Kernels keep through the lean winter, hard and golden. To be corn is to be sharp and sturdy. To hold power latent in a capsule; to burst in starchy explanation from a singed hull. Corn is patient, careful; gives up its nourishment only in magic preparations, lime and water, fire.

Around the smudgy bonfire, they all mimic Luz. How she was reaching, not for apples or pears, but in a crazy yearning, for the call in her spine. They make a dance of it, the swaying up, and Luz laughs; the fire paints them gold and orange. They call it her corn dance, and Luz joins in, adds a playful shriek and wail. The men recline and wind around the edges, sit and clap, call out teases. When the women get a little drunk, they do Luz's corn dance, flinging down and up, and almost feel like they remember.

At night when they lie still, trying to uncoil, the women imagine their spines stretching and straightening in jointed segments. Their feet fusing end-to-end at the heels, toes spreading long and thin, pale. They dream what it is like to be planted, not moving endlessly like a cloud of yellow pollen on the wind. They hold a body-memory of endurance; where the grandmother grinds corn in her grandmother's stone. Corn was the gift, a picture of their bodies' striving.

The women come from many places. Their names are Luz, Fernanda, Marie-Jeanne, Sonia, Kathie, Olivia, Odette, Yrma, Pearl, Lacey. The sun fires them different shades of brown. No matter what their language of memory, at night they all have the same vision: a wisp of light unfurling from the base of bent spine; a gift, something prized, something worth saving. They would rather be tall, durable, planted. In dreams they stand upright, doing a crazy dance, while the men and children curl supple and laughing at their feet. The pollen in their bellies is calling. Women who dream of corn.

What the Body Learns

Tossed and crumpled bodies of young men litter the field like dirty rags. A pile disentangles limb from limb; they creak and huff stiffly to their feet, reborn immortals, tug muddy jerseys into place, adjust pads, bang clods out of cleats. Warm-tinted lights bleed their colors gray. Into formation across the line of scrimmage, and again, crash of plastic and thuds of flesh on flesh. The same boys who struggle with the razor, call out choral come-ons, whose dismayed mothers make them wash their semen-stained sheets themselves, the same boys who lean on lockers, who save up money to buy used cars that they gun past the school. They dare harm, take impact in the chest, in the leg-bone, and fall.

Crushed forms like tatters on the field then they scramble up again, smiling, cursing, dead warriors restored by magic dragon's teeth, and the girls in the stands point and wave. In the bleachers or with the pompons, they cheer, whisper and giggle; watching is their only option in this game. The girls love these boys whose bodies are sound as apples, flesh solid and sweet. With hands and eyes, they love the grooves and hollows of the boy bodies—gully along the outer thigh, round of the deltoid, slopes of the pecs. The girls compare against their own bodies, where even taut muscles are mostly curved and smoothed, softened. They covet the boys, their weight and density, power, their envied conformation, gleeful immortality. The boys' bodies have magic. Girls are greedy. If the girls can't have such strength and magic, they will melt into it and steal it that way.

The girls' new bodies betray them at every turn. The moments that used to be transcendent, glorious, now always seem cut short. In grade school, they were even. A girl could win, in the fifty-yard dash, to the top of the climbing rope. She could push him away, sometimes best him in a sand-lot scuffle, a tangle of elbows and scarred knees. Girls and boys as teammates on the court, laughing and teasing, the body an honest and neutral thing. By junior high, that had changed. Feminine fat that just won't shed costs them hundredths of seconds at the finish line, costs them second glances from the boys. They try pills, cigarettes, laxatives. Cramps lean like dull fists in front of their kidneys. Now the girls learn that difference arises from their new bodies, is their power and their weakness; the field will not be level again until they are old, old women whose beaked faces and lank hair makes them indistinguishable from old men. Their new bodies seem to ask things beyond their owners' permission. Just by existing, breasts and buttocks, tan legs, seem to draw stares and touches, even when arms fold tight shut, skirts are long and weighty. They might as well learn to use it. They might as well unlock the secrets.

They herd, those girls whose new bodies attract the eyes of other kids' fathers. They clump at under-age shows. They rove the malls in pairs and packs, trying on clothes, decorate and display their forms in long mirrors. After shopping, they huddle over sodas, five in a narrow booth. Someone reaches for the french fries, someone gets a refill; they pinch flesh at the navel, calculate how much ass is enough, what kind of jeans are acceptable this year. Thin or athletic, vivacious or studious, a jellybean assortment sharing the same questions:

—What does it mean when a boy says 'we should get together'? Like, is that a date or a hook-up?

—Have you ever had a bikini wax?

—No way, I bet it hurts too much.

—But if you act friendly, pass the ketchup, people call you a flirt, and if you don't, the guys say you're stuck up; what am I supposed to do?

—I'm not lettin' no boy see my nipples, I got good bras.

—He practically put his tongue down my throat, that part was gross.

—What about bra straps under a tank top?

—Oh, but he's sooo cute, every time I hear this song it makes me think of him, I swear.

—They don't like competing with girls, so does that

mean you should let them win?

Some milk-fed daydream in them wants to be finally noticed and possessed, to be renamed—but only by the desired one. They sense that what the body learns is the key to this new world, the key to getting, keeping, avoiding boys, that somehow this gateway is crucial. Some advocate passivity, soft voices, others push the direct approach, but they all agree—it's in the body. Those whose desire doesn't feel the male magnet are doubly puzzled. The girls are anxious to figure it out before some unfathomed deadline arrives.

The girl walking home from school hates the new body. It aches, it sways, it distorts her clothes, it sprouts dark coiled hair. It sprouts constraints and restrictions. Deodorant. Shaving. Don't swim while you're having it. Pimple cream. She learns to fold her arms over chest, to slump, when they look at her like that. Freedoms snatched away, her mother's new suspiciousness, frowns and sniffing, a new nosiness into her things, her whereabouts. *I don't want you going out with that junk on your face. I don't care what other kids wear, that looks trampy.* The mother's eye expects betrayal, is waiting. The girl calls her body traitor. It has gone off on its own, disjunct from her spirit, divides her even from her mother. No good can come of this change.

Junior high boys know the ambivalence of transition. To shift the focus, take control, they prod the backs of T-shirts for tell-tale bands and hooks, snap straps, stare pointedly at the bulging busts, tease cruelly, sneak a hand to their own crotches when they think no one's looking. They pass made-up stories about what happens at parties—thudding words that take on life—*puts out, frigid, easy, ugly, pig.* Even at that age, when their beards haven't quite started but pimples have, before they have the advantage of size, somehow they know the rules are changing, the importance of taking the upper hand. They side against their female former teammates from park board soccer or basketball teams—girls whose flat chests mirrored their own and who ripped off jerseys to trade, girls next door. The girls at first learn silence, then take up the gauntlet, verbal parries and put-downs, guerilla tactics. They try to decipher the odd, shifting power of bodies. They learn open longing is a stain, tuck away desires until sent for.

By fourteen or fifteen, name-calling is replaced by the puzzle of hiding and revealing desires. A girl beneath a boy on the couch somehow knows this: his body's imperative is hers, that it isn't a matter for speech or reckoning when his hands push her sweater up and glide over her ribs toward her bra, when his convex thighs press into hers, when their tongues tangle. Her body wants the same as his. As they clasp and fumble, the girl wonders if from now on, her body is allowed only answers, only yes or no, not how much, when, what—no questions without being a rebel in this new order. Her tongue, her hip, her yes. Her body learns these answers on the couch, and posed to advantage against the hallway lockers, dancing with swivel of hips and shoulders in the gym. The power of choosing and being chosen, the hidden code revealed through her body. Yes and no, its new powers.

In the library, another girl has swallowed *No* whole,

made it hers. Her rectangular body leans in rigid remonstrance over her book, her pencil-strokes taking command. She says No to her body's betrayal, its too-round breasts, the dark ugly nipples, the curving hips. Her mouth stays No, refusing to open beyond the diameter of a straw: sips of water; curled, translucent slices of cucumber. She will master this runaway flesh of hers, animal self that seems to call out for stares and touches she doesn't want, a body she didn't ask for, autonomous and negated. She will make it bend to her ideals. Wants back those slender boy hips, anonymous flat chest, her freedom. Six miles a day, sometimes more, with hard flat paces she runs the softening flesh right off it, pounds stairs, crunches the hated belly into a circumflex. She lies, she evades, to keep reign over this terror, her flesh. She hides a dwindling body behind docility, loose sweaters, straight A's, a tidy bedroom, glee club, workouts. Her parents call her a model of discipline: they are so proud, so proud. Her control, pen gripped tightly in one hand, holds No firmly lodged in her throat.

There's a girl in somebody's parent's study. In other rooms, she'd say she is an athlete, her legs are sound. She'd say her hair is brown and swept from her face, her handwriting is neat. In other rooms, she has a voice. But in somebody's parent's study, as the party beyond blares and blurs, she's the girl who wants the body of the boy. At first she liked his face, his build, some look in his eye that made her desirable. She liked his smell and the touch of his hand in the small of her back as they slipped away from dark rooms of beer, smoke, dancing. Now, this brown-haired girl, this athlete, she wants the hands that grip her waist, her thighs, the bruising thumbs. She wants to possess tensile strength of his legs, solid chest that won't yield to her pushing. His skin is smooth and durable as cowhide, it will not mark from her flimsy flailing nails, tiny knuckles. She stumbles against a desk. He has wavy brown hair and a button-down shirt. Prints on the wall tilt and slide. If she had this boy's body, as massive, as impermeable, she would not stumble in beery stupor, she would not lose her balance. Her voice would not skitter under the furniture, unheard. If she had that body, he would not be able do what he is doing, tugging at her skirt, forcing apart her legs and pinning her while the room spins, bending over her back, pushing her face into somebody's parent's desk while his penis scrapes against her and his breath claws at her ear. She doesn't want to be that body, pinned. How thin the thread between no and yes, her voice spinning away with the room, whose body, the lost meaning of possession.

In the locker room, a pale girl can't stop throwing up. She hides in the toilet stall. The bell has rung, the others are gone. That pale, blonded body's betrayal is complete down to her guts. There is little to come up but still some unfurling reflex surges and retches. She has no explanation yet, does not know a parasite has turned her body into host, planted in her some tiny life that already feeds, commandeers her hormones and makes her spit. She makes no connection between sour stomach and her body's new powers to say, come here, pick me. His name is Joey, and they hold hands between classes, trade love songs pulled from MP3s, whisper in the back of Spanish class, get it on in his room while his mom's at work. The bell has already rung and her street clothes are still in her locker. The queasiness lingers but there's nothing left in her buckling stomach. The floor is dusty blue tile. The others are all gone, and she is late for second period.

Even the tall, confident ones, the ones who know the body's place, have to crack the code each time. The popular junior wants to be a doctor. She wants to peel apart skins and cut away cancers, remove wayward growths, clamp and splice arteries, mend ruptures of the flesh. The body, all its fascinations, cities, freeways, garbage dumps, power plants: the body. She wants to win the debate meet, and bike along the coast someday. Her body is proud; admires its own shape in the mirror, approves of its curves and planes, clothes it with care, babies its nutmeg-brown skin, keeps it from harm. This body knows bodies are a medium of exchange, even now, when it's a personal transaction. Right now, her body wants the boys in their two-tone letter jackets, wants that particular flesh leaning against the locker, one particular smile, wants to wrap its hands and lips and legs around that particular body more than anything else. Some brainy flood of chemicals shakes cocktails of soppy daydreams, a want that addles her mind, tingles her skin. Unwieldy desire throws her off. She knows the proper rituals, knows how to make it easy for him—a lingering look, a smile, a question, a compliment; glossed lips, a clinging shirt, a confident pose. What if it's not enough? Maybe he likes black girls, white girls, petite, mousy, overly vivacious. She'll consult with girlfriends, buy clothes. She'll rehearse the confident supplication; her power is to somehow elicit that question to which the answer is yes, and make that body surrender, a specimen to her dissecting longings.

Invulnerable, the boys seem—even tall, skinny ones, ones with bad complexions, the shy ones. Boys hold their balance at the breastbone, walk and calibrate gravity from that keel, a little top-heavy, so that they look awkward dancing with the supple, hip-focused girls. Girls imagine the boys hold their power in clean unconsciousness, swinging it from this pivot-point, neither arrogant nor ashamed. Does it all come from that difference of the body, its size, its strength? Boys don't know the fear they cause when a loud gang trails a girl down a dark street—or do they? Unaware, monopolize classroom conversation. With the confidence of rulers, they take for granted that everything is built to their specs: cars, auditorium seats, tall gym lockers, handtools, levers on fire doors, soccer cleats. Modifications are made from this master template, male body, and all else is merely scaled down, not refitted. Even the dating game seems tailored to male action. The first dark whisperings of sex. Orchestrated from boy's tongue, boy's balance.

The girls love the boys' bodies for this preeminence. Adoring and envious of their newly diverged flesh, its new hulls and fenders. Self-confidence and satisfaction will come later, for the lucky. They do what they can to keep up, fit in. Slowly they learn female arts and strategies: glimmer-sheens on their skins, undulating gazelle motions, mask of selfhood from a perfumed magazine, mastering their discrete circle of powers. The girls will try to make friends with their own bodies so their flesh can befriend the boys'. Immortal, smashproof, insistent on the seething grass field, bodies that won't fail and flab, muscled bodies that sometimes please but anyway, bodies the girls can borrow, rags dropped on the field, then theirs to coax or punish behind the bleachers. With permission's glow the girls admire their own bodies through the boys' eyes: mysterious and scented, tantalizing, luscious, their perishable bodies made promising and potent, exotic new lands waiting to be claimed. They love the boys wild, their huffing abandon, slippery kisses, hard grip that lets the girls be hard, urgent and deathless, too.

Girls do a lot of hoping. A lot of waiting. The body is learning the way to wholeness and sometimes it pays a price. Boys get to call their own bodies *home.*

The girls, latent and fierce, polished, curious, will sneak that magic somehow.

Breath

And in this harsh world draw thy breath in pain,
To tell my story.
–Shakespeare, *Hamlet*

1

The moon's eye is wide.
Less than whole, it stares through a tattered web of cloud. Nearly autumn; nearly night; I am nearly here. My breath eludes me. Ghostly, unfleshed—tight, ebbing. Snatched away by some sudden thief, a swirl of ghosts and memories. I count my breaths. Slowly. Alone. It only happens when I'm alone—no one to tell, no ear to hear. I am trying to hold air in place, to fill. To calm, to ease: *you, body, behave.* Holding, but it slides past, only a mouthful, can't fill, can't keep them here, I can't catch up.

2

Break the surface of water, breath sucked deep. Wavelet breath of sleep. The breath of fire, oxygen debt, as muscles seize. Quick breathing of passion. Sighs, sobs, exclamations. Counting breaths.

3

I try to fix on facts, other moments, other years. It takes such discipline—breathing—once a panic comes and air slips from my lips the way so many other things slip from grasp. *Behave, you lungs.* Thoughts to calm my anxious gasps. Holidays, vacations, cheer. Eight years old: The first time I really know about breathing. A rodeo in Louisville, vacation with my cousins. At eight, I love the horses, want to be horse, rider, speed, sweat. Brown dust flying round the barrel racers in the arena, the lickety-split of their turns, chaps flapping, tails whipping. Then it starts: the slow squeezing in my chest. I don't have words to describe my body's betrayal. Drowning, I squeak and scrape like a sea-thing in the foreign air. Body going its own way without me, spooked horse. My aunt squints: What's wrong with you? My cousins whine at being rushed away; I feel guilty for my whining lungs.

A doctor gives me medicine that makes me whir and spin, says I'm allergic to the animals, pollen-dusting trees, explains my body's overreaction. Drugs silence my wheeze but free other voices within me, mind spinning, spinning. I swing my leg like a pendulum from the side of the bed in my aunt's rosy guest room and my brother in the next bed yells, Quiet! Adrenaline whips my mind in figure-eights. But I breathe without realizing—unconsciously, naturally.

4

The first time I hear her laugh, I think we'll be friends. A big laugh with a bright, sharp edge, a laugh that slices. My freshman year: in the dorm sunroom, I hear music. A girl with brown hair that I'd seen around has her guitar on her lap. She is picking, and she tells me to join in, starts explaining something from choir. When I try to "sing from my diaphragm" like she told me to, I squeak; her bright peals ring around the room, and soon I'm laughing, too. Margaret says, keep that up and I'll have to call you Olive Oyl. Do that, I say, and I'll have to call you Brutisk. I'm learning a song by the Lemonheads, she says, wanna hear? That's how I think of her laugh, a singer's laugh, strong as a trumpet.

5

I count breaths. Incoming breath slowly opens the petals of the lotus. Exhalations close. Deep pink water-lily, folding, unfolding. Let it float in your chest: a blossom resolved from steam, steam created from water. Water in your abdomen heated by a ball of golden light, created from a ball of red light, which joins with fire; fire heats water, makes steam, steam resolves into the lotus.

That routine forms the slow poetry of chi gong. It helps at times like this. After one long shriek of a year, I'll try anything to find calm, to go back to the body. Chi gong class meets in the science center amid chalk boards and sealed windows. The instructor's voice is calm, precise. The huge concrete building sighs and groans through giant cylindrical ducts that traverse the high ceiling. An hour as just an hour, when I don't feel helpless. Counting. Going, going, gone.

Perch on the edge of a hard plastic chair, hold palms up before the belly. The voice is a bell, a pulse. In the whole-body breathing method, use all the pores of the body to take in light, energy, colors, sensations. Opening, closing. The building sighs. The blossom closes, keeping in all the lights, sensations, inspirations. Sip as soft and cleanly as an infant. Make your breath subtle. Count your breaths. Try to let go. And there is the lotus, always opening and folding shut.

6

Memories so fresh, they confuse me: so present, so unwilling to take their seats in the past, dreams with the texture of life. Inhale. Things I hold on to: The first time I kissed Ted he smelled faintly of vanilla. Exhale. The way you can breathe while you're kissing though it seems you shouldn't, like a practiced swimmer's rhythm.

I reach for the good ones, like the late-summer day Margaret and Ted and I go to the Cajun music festival. Margaret and I are still roomies; we hop in my boyfriend's big old LeSabre and drive down to the Stepping Stone Ranch. Three stages, lawn seating, sun and yellow-jackets everywhere. Ted calls them garbage bees. Here they are in the golden haze of dust-filled air, two of the people I love best: Ted, wiry, quiet and tousle-headed, tapping the toe of his shoe; Margaret, in my blue gauze shirt, tossing her shining black hair as she dances, the bright metal of her laugh. This is the harvest moment, in the pitch of our laughter, the brush of his warm hand on my neck—we're sated, ripe. She likes the fiddle contest best, the way boots stomp on boards, and I'd scuff rhythm on a washboard. In the gold-striped tent, we learn bouncy Cajun dance steps; Ted takes turns dancing with each of us, bounce-bounce-bounce-knee-up, till we're winded. Later, C.J. Chenier's on the main stage and we kick up plenty of dust and bees, laughing. You can't sit still for zydeco, and somehow I get stung on my arm. Margaret holds ice cubes on my skin and it turns into another joke.

There's a huge September sun and we're buzzed on overpriced cheap beer and we're untouchable, bellowing along with everyone else, *laisse' les bon temps roulez!* Ted keeps twining fingers in my hair, putting his arm around my shoulders, Margaret sings. They happily suck the goo out of the crawdads rattling in a paper basket, but I don't. Even with bees and dust, the last-of-summer sunburns, it's the perfect day. On the way home, Billy Joel's song "Uptown Girl" comes on the classic-rock station and Margaret and I crack up. Remembering a recent party and a drunk friend, we sing, She's an upchuck girl! Tired of living in a White Russian world, over and over. We laugh our fool heads off, and Ted nods and says, You two deserve each other.

7

You, body, behave. Sharp, noisy intake: I order it to stop. This room is too tight. I think I've learned some kind of control over this body. I thought I'd learned some kind of control over this body and its rebellions much younger—the wheeze recalls another moment, and I lecture my younger self, order that younger body around. At sixteen, that body hasn't yet met hardship, believes in mastery. Prideful thing, at the park it runs wind-sprints along the marked field in the deepening dusk, counting out yards: 25, 50, 100 yards, 60 seconds and do it again. High school junior, a starter on the soccer team this year, push. Jog, sprint, jog. Tough body, you run timed quarter-miles against your brother Nick. Legs good and hard. Despite a blast from the inhaler, shy tunnels of bronchi in the lungs begin to close in protest. They have cause. Occasional asthma—no alarm. You are willful and you run until you bray like a mule.

He says, Come on, again! You start, will not give in.
to fronds of ragweed that grow palm-fingered along the
tracks and alleys. You pull up mid-sprint, hee-haw. can't
speak.   Want to cry from clawing discomfort.
can't spare the air. Nick says, come on, one more.   You
shake your.   head and plod down the path.
squeaking deep.   along the freeway wall, home.
But the panic, like this panic, will fade   and
you will   do it again tomorrow.

8

Now I've learned to breathe the pain away, certain pains of the body. A deep intake then long, slow, hissing release, the ache in my muscles flying out my lips. It helps for the agony of a massage, the strife of a hard hill run. My body adopts these pains, keeps effects, forgets causes. Between my shoulder blades, muscles taut and hanging on for dear life, a massage therapist's thumbs dig in: spasm. I push the air out again, a long groan without voice, as fingers burrow and the frond of muscle hoards its own resilience, tensed. I focus on the counting. Exhale, relax. That's the theory. Her fingers bully and cajole. I whoosh out the pain as best I can, a desperate balance between tension and release, almost like sex, and finally fibers yield with a little side-to-side slip and a noiseless pop. I try to focus on sounds of breath in my head, feel of air in my mouth, like when running uphill, the inhale-exhale, eyes on the sky, feeling only my face, not aching legs. It goes on for an hour. On the worst knots I can't help it, I cry out.

9

Goose of a girl, you distrust it when Ted uses the L-word too soon—clear on that, *too soon*. But his affection is a big soft bed and you want to lie there a while. He believes you are beautiful, so then you are. After a while, when he says the L-word, it feels as real as the staves and gunwales of his flesh. As something in the fibers of your tendons, real as carbon, as protein—organic, like breathing. It's been a year already when he leaves for the mountains: See an old friend, just a couple weeks. What do you say, so confident, comfortable? You're remembering a trip to the San Juans when you were fourteen, thin air and glory, looking down on mountaintops, on the sky; once adjusted to the height, you climbed and climbed. Silly girl, you wish him bright skies, good climbing.

Ted goes, but no calls—first, a gentle worry, then a slight nausea you push away. The first letter is six weeks later, with no return address—Waiting list for P.O. boxes, he writes. Margaret consoles you: Aw, you know guys—no concept of time. She takes you out for ice cream. The next letter takes a month and shudders with hurtful explanation. That's the first time you felt it implode in your chest, a vacuum-blossom, sucking out all the air, a panic chiming through limbs. Oh, you think, searching for an unused inhaler: altitude sickness.

10
The shift of a vowel sound, a lesson from high school French. *Tu souffles*: you breathe, or you whisper. *Tu siffles*, you wheeze. One immunologic prompt, one shy molecular shift. You, body, overreacting.

11
I recall that weight on my belly. A big orange cat, a fourteen-pounder with tufted cheeks, painted face, white boots. He adopted me, a conqueror casually waving his flag, brazenly crept into my lap on the porch and claimed me. Margaret says, He's a sweetie, are you gonna keep him? Since I'm living solo now, I think, why not? Each night when I'm almost asleep, he bounds onto the bed with a chirp, pushes his shape against me, scents fingers with his whiskers. Bossy, insistent. He purrs, so absolutely delighted each night to find this warm, miraculously safe place. Sometimes, despite being such different creatures, I think we breathe in rhythm for a moment, and fall asleep.

12
In, out, focus. I lose track, I can't fix months, only mea-

sure by presence and absence what came before, what comes after; beginning and end are a matter of reckoning. Funny how present an absence can be. Counting, a progression, syntax. Trying to track, the image I pluck is a morning hard-cornered with rain when the surgeon strides out, a woman with a gray-streaked ponytail; a creased, tan face set off by green scrubs. The lines around her mouth are carved deeply. She had come with good recommendations. Margaret's sister takes notes and her eyelids swell and whites redden. Then she explains to us, with her nurse's precision, the masses, the biopsy, the prognosis.

I lie, claiming to be another sister, to get into the recovery room. This is a ride I don't want to be on and I'm getting dizzy. Every essential thing about Margaret is reduced to her form in a star-spangled johnny. She is so stoned from anesthesia that she's gleeful about those organs left untouched, not understanding why. I love you, I love you, she says drunkenly to each one of us. She clasps our hands, beaming like the birthday girl at the end of the party.

13

Keep counting. Visualize the lotus unfolding. Here and now, belly rising. Try to understand what's passed. Past. And present. Don't think about the squeak, a metal shelf cutting off inhalation. In, round like the moon. Now. Easy. Opening, closing.

14

Sooner than expected, my sister-in-law gets pregnant.

The grannies-to-be are all a-twitter, crochet needles and sewing machine, respectively, flying at high speed. The expectant couple doesn't announce it till Andrea, my aerobics-hopping sister-in-law, starts to show thickening at the middle. My brother Nick keeps revising lists of names, which I shoot down: Benjamin? Overused. Sophronia? Too highfalutin. Dorcas? Now, that's just ugly. His wife is wrapped up in the changes to her body—changes in the texture of her hair, her swelling middle, and later on, a dark stripe up her belly like an old C-section scar. I feel possessed, she says, me and not me. I can feel the hips go wide, and I get winded—climbing stairs is a mini-workout, this kid's already demanding.

15

It's a cool night, a good night for sleeping. Animate air stirs, swirls through leaves and twigs, grasses and fences, silently gives them voice.

All sorts of antagonists are a-flight tonight: it hasn't rained in weeks. Powdered molds, dust, grass pollen, ghosts of fertility, a prairie full of pollen-asteroids and land-mines. Mast cells are ready to smash and explode when the offending microns meet eyes, nose, ready to drown the intruders and flood you, traitor body.

I lie in bed and make up names: BEFORE, AFTER, to accommodate one long shriek of a year. This after-life of gone, gone, gone. So how do I make sense of it? I go on. Continuance is in the blood, animal-self instincts, the struggle for air. The mind weaves a net around things one can't understand, the losses, all of it. Finds a way to tell it, spins unnourishing straw into gold. Tries to make reason out of scattered puzzle pieces.

In this AFTER life, my body's been keeping clean. Been staying put in the filtered air, singing along to the hum. Breath, a clean virtue. But I miss the company of night.

I slide open the door to the tiny balcony and sounds rush in with cool, gentle air: crickets, leaves, train whistle. Soft sound and shudder of night. An unfelt breeze barely lifts the hem of undrawn curtains, pulses slats of the blinds so they sway. Unplug the humming air filter, my bedroom chaperone, open the bedroom window, admit all those longed-for ghosts. Like any long night with a lover, it may leave me exhausted and headached in the morning. But I've been too long without this company, breathing side by side with the late-summer night.

16

Starts slow: murmured words, little gasps, kisses. Fleshy palmings, skin speaks first, conversation of arms, buttocks, legs, hollows of collarbone, shoulder blades, neck. Fingers questioning. Muscles start to clench, faint sheen of sweat bursts out. Both working toward the same thing, together and self-involved. The body saves some special voices for these moments, a taxonomy of noises, colored outrushes of breath; someone groans, the other mews, demanding, breathing hard now, grunts and cries: crescendo.

Recovery: hammering hearts, breathless, then breathing, then breath; breath, returning, returning from wherever it was, slower; here; I. Am. I.

17
Breath, death. Elemental alchemy.
Respire, expire. Life's lover, inspiration.

18
When is it that she calls me with the news? I lose track. Joys and pains that swirl and dance like pollens; dear ones who vanish like steam from warm lungs. I can look to the moon for answers but its memory only lasts a month. I know it's late, dirty winter when her doctors' visits start: the slushy streets, heavy coats. Memory hinges on odd markers; dates don't stick in my head. A brother married the year you had mono. The Twins won the Series the year I started that job. But what numerals, what contexts affix to these events? People remember catastrophe: Blizzard of '78, Flood of '96. Margaret must be pinned to something else in life besides Margaret, some pin to fix her in the resin of time—or did her illness swallow the months?

19
ABC: airway, breathing, circulation. Basic survey. If pulse but no breathing, begin mouth-to-mouth resuscitation. Five quick breaths into alcohol-sour rubber lips. Check again. If no pulse, begin cardiopulmonary resuscitation, breaths and compressions. Do not stop until relieved by another rescuer. In case of blocked airway, try the Heimlich maneuver, or rotate victim and thump between shoulder blades with base of the palm. If the obstruction cannot be cleared, make a short incision a thumb's breadth below

the larynx. Remove the ink apparatus from a stick-pen and insert the hollow barrel into incision as a tracheal airway. Proceed with artificial respiration.

The mannequin's rubber lids lack lashes, will never open. Chest compressions squeak and thunk her rubber rib-cage. Sometimes breaths whistle if the mouth seal is not complete. These days, all rescue professionals carry ambu-bags; no telling what's carried in any unspeaking mouth.

20

Then the fall day the orange cat calls for me, my furred familiar, hyperventilating on the floor. My heart races, too. After the exam and chest films, the after-hours vet is ready to send us home, but I know better. The cat butts his head into my ribs, his almost-normal breathing taking comfort from my smell, my warmth; clinging, begging. Yet I trust another, put him in the carrier. As I fill out carbon paper-work, the cat gives a long yowl, last air of life escaping; still magnificent, vomits with a wave that rocks his length, goes limp. They bag him, try to breathe for him, but his heart had stopped talking.

Margaret comes over and she cries with me. We rinse the vomit-stained carrier in the tub. First man, now cat, gone. Sometimes he used to sleep draped across my stomach, blissful, possessive, a fourteen-pound fur that subdued my breath with his warm weight. Now breathless.

Is it true they come in threes?

21
Out. In. Out, a plume, a spout. A faraway child in a blue-swirled swimsuit, almost somebody else. At twelve, a good swimmer. Count to four. Arms pull, pull, batter, splatter, but it's not there for the taking. First you have to lift your face from the water, suck in, kick again, pull four more strokes, hurtling toward that next breath, always behind, lurching up for that next inhalation, oxygen deficit starts to build in your muscles, they want to slow but you can't, you need to get to that next breath and the only way to do it is to grapple, to pull like you've never pulled, you would voice the strain but you can't, and the next, slap the tiled wall and your teammate leaves the block and there you hang, face up at last, sucking and gasping. Trying to fill. The reason you finally quit: those at-tears moments hanging on the gutter, the gasping break, the moment when you gulp chlorinated bilge the wrong way, finding ancestral panic housed in cells and muscles.

22
My sister-in-law grows huge. There's no place to put that baby in the short span between ribs and hips; it rides out front like a basketball. We do the baby shower buffet style, since there's no bellying up to table. She's throned in a streamered chair. He's a kicker. She's too tiny—has to pee often, feels always short of breath, can only eat a half-cup of food at at time. No room for baby, lungs, stomach, bladder, liver all at once. Joking, we say, That's to make you think labor is a relief.

23

She's not doing well, and we all know how it goes from here. Margaret dwindles. It has her by the liver, the diaphragm, the colon. We take her to the country, to her sister's farm. Blue skies, children—the border collie follows Margaret's little nephew, cleaning up the trail of Cheerios. Blossoms riot in the yard, peonies and lupines, columbines, snapdragons. She likes to sit on the sagging sofa facing out the hayloft door. Margaret's smile turns bony. We curl close and cry wearily and watch the storms move up the valley. We trade stories and laugh: remember Cajun dancing? The Peter Gabriel concert? That bad haircut? Remember how the cat slept belly-up? Now she likes to hold my hand. Peonies nod their heads above a round glass jar. She sleeps sitting up now, and breathing is painful; it's time for morphine. We've done all the goodbye stuff. She wants to make plans, give away necklaces, CDs, photos. She hopes they can fix her up enough for an open casket. She wants to call it a day.

24

You must pace yourself to hold off night. What terrifies me most in nightmares is when I can't cry out—in fear, in warning. No air, no voice, just hoarse effort, utter failure. Without breath, speech, we die, or wake.

25

Sophomore year of college: I've run too hard perhaps, and acrid blasts from the inhaler haven't helped. I'm used to wheeze and squeak, but it's tightening up too fast—never like this, never like this. Each one a labor. Roommate, wave her over, no time to be cool—squeak out, Hospital. Not even really wheezing. just shutting off. In the car, Margaret looks at me, anxious. Panic fires my entire body. won't help. if no airway. lightheaded. Suffocation?

Adrenaline? Can't tell, elemental. panic has me. for the first time it occurs to me. I could die and. Why did nobody tell me? never passed out before. Never

strange pictures vision starting to.

what love? bleach and. the thing I think. of,

wistfully, is:

26

Hospital trips, good and bad. She pants, she shrieks, she groans. The breath is doing all the work; that's why they practiced so much, in the hospital lounge on the tawny rug, with their pillows and other couples all around, whooshing and grunting. WOOHHHH! She can't take in enough air to push as hard as she needs to. The baby is in the way; she hasn't breathed fully in weeks, only diet rations, little Dixie-cups of air. She imagines the air pushing it out instead, a gale wind, not the too-dense muscle straining away. She'd roar more if she could. Get it OOOOUT. She is still breathing for them both and not until she stops huffing and yelling will the baby have its turn to wail.

27

In. Out.

It is all around, *chi*, life-force, you just have to drink

it in, open pores, admit. Inspire, from Latin *inspirare*, to breathe into. See also Spirit; French *esprit* from Latin *spiritus*, breath, from *spirare*, to breathe. You, body.

God, imagination, life, wonder.

28

There was little left of Margaret but her shrink-wrapped bones, her defiant spirit hovering stubbornly around her bald and shapely head, her eyeballs turned up, evasive; the too-slow, autonomic breaths. Too few per minute as we counted. And now I have to learn to use the past tense. She *loved* all sorts of music and to pig out on ice cream. Chocolate fudge brownie. Janis Joplin and Billy Joel. Her laughter, anger and tears *were* titanic. Her hair *had been* smooth and lustrous black before it left her. She *was*.

I was the last to arrive; a sober, six-hour drive to the farm. High summer. She was waiting for me, they said. So I sat on the arm of the chair that had become her home, held her smooth, yellow fingers, and said goodbye. Whispered permission. She was twenty-nine and must have weighed sixty-five pounds. Her breathing had been getting more prickly for weeks, a permanent stitch in her side as the patch on her diaphragm flourished, liver cells overreacted. Her breaths were loud, rare, a thin thread tethering her wandering spirit to that body.

All around, the ones she loved: boyfriend, sisters, parents, friends. We sang to her until after midnight. She waited until we bedded down on sofas and carpets, began our own slowing breath of night, a slowly sighing choir, until the one hour when her last listening sister succumbed, until we'd turned our backs, and she quietly stopped.

29
Some cool bright mornings, when the sun is sleeping low on the horizon and has no hard stare, I run invisibly, solo. I am gifted with strong and relaxed stride, almost effortless, sipping at the air like dainty drinks of water, and the rhythmic rise and fall of my belly seems easy, as if to stop would be an affront to nature.

30
When this panic centers in my lungs, cause or effect? It's a new thing, this gasping that comes upon me in a quiet moment. Perhaps a primal fear my reason won't admit; instinctual response, the ache of a ghost-limb. Quick flutter of forgetting and remembrance. I should be blooming. I, who have life and breath, a mandate to speak, should be living broad and tall, fiery, a tigress. But here in life AFTER, sometimes it comes out of nowhere, even when I'm at rest. Some microscopic trigger, perhaps the disappeared voices, and a vacuum blossoms—a frantic tightness—sudden sting of a preliminary wheeze, seizing. I try to submit, give in—survivors yield, a jellyfish float. Panic takes you under. I try to breathe light and slow, fill the space. To picture the lotus blooming. Count slowly. I imagine the cat curled against me. I try to peel memory from its pain and hold the colors of joy. Outside, I watch the low and heavy moon, almost full and yellow, neither one of us quite whole. Slow those breaths.

I count.

I try to remember sureness within my flesh, the forever of an embrace, all doubt and demons banished, sweetness. To recall ease and ignorance. I can hold only now.

The moon changes, round, a mouth, I am, and there is only breathing.

The Nameless Season

Dad is going down to the basement again. The look on his face is stony—a stoic expression we're used to seeing on each other's faces at this time of year.

February, the fickle month, the one that should have been named for the two-faced god. The time when we look back in fear, look forward in hope. It's been six years and we've learned to stick by names of months, avoid the painful reference to seasons. This is the month when the Gulf Stream darts back and forth, treating us to frigid wind chills, wet snows, and alluring thaws. The birds that are left, birds that can come and go if this place fails, begin songs of territory and enticement. The season of nerves and apprehension. Come February, we cluster at the windows, stare anxiously at trees and exposed patches of earth amid the snow, helplessly waiting to learn our fate. Often, Dad heads to the basement.

February once meant cross-country skiing or longing for

warm vacations. Mom would dog-ear the pages of her seed catalogs and Dad might go to the Home and Garden Show to pinch hoses and eye hammocks and edging. My sister Laura would skate at the park or lie on the sofa, thumbing through her fashion magazines for spring trends, and I'd fret over choosing a summer camp, because the deposit was due. February was an over-hyped Valentine's Day and maybe a President's Day ski weekend; snowstorms, and days when we thrilled at the sun's growing heat on our faces.

That was when four seasons organized our lives with a predictability too basic for us to see. Now, we watch the slow drip of a Tuesday thaw and stare at the impossibly tiny buds, waiting to learn if spring will come this year.

The dead years are terrible. The first one came when I was twelve. One cold night, someone awakened to a strange sound—perhaps a sleet storm. A soft rattle, a thudding. Then the morning recognition, my mother's and father's anxious voices in the bedroom. "What on earth . . . ?" Daybreak revealed a dark carpet over icy yards and sidewalks, the browny-green nap crushed into a slick mat on the roads. Birds picked inquisitively at the tough detritus. My father put on his jacket over his pjs and stepped into his boots and out the door; he picked up a handful of brown stuff, then stroked cold fingers over a barren branch of forsythia. "Caroline?" he said to my mother, and the note of awe and fear in his voice had us clamoring, "What, what is it?" Along the street we could see the porch lights go on; neighbor called to neighbor. Wonder turned to alarm at something we'd never seen before. Dad hurried indoors and shut the door tight, and said "Girls, follow me."

We ran for radios and internet newscasts, as a new and terrible dread sprouted within us. Later, we learned it was no nuclear or chemical attack, as we all feared in those first awful hours. Now we all recognize the sound of anguish that sends us running for windows and porches, where we shiver in our nightclothes and sob—the sound of a drumming heavier than rain, with all the icy repercussions of winter: the leaf-buds hailing to the ground.

That awful year, the sun grew warmer and warmer on our skin, as it always had; the earth kept tilting, but there was nothing green to leaf, no flower-spindles from the maples or crocus from the ground. Rains yielded only mud. We packed away our parkas and boots, and learned to wear brimmed hats after our first sunburns; there was no real shade beyond the man-made, only stark planks of shadow from tree trunks and limbs. Sales of patio umbrellas boomed at first, but no one wanted to sit out with the yards all bare and brown. A few tough and fibrous weeds struggled along until late May, and then shriveled. No one knew what was happening, so we were saddled with precautions. Still, my mom kept the bird bath filled for a while, even after the water rationing started.

"This is what it's like down South all the time," my sister Laura said one day, as she lay on the wood floor with a moist cloth on her forehead and her sandy hair fanned away from her neck. "Sweltering. Tin roofs and no A.C." Temps in the 80s sometimes happened in late May, but this time there was no respite from the sun's eye.

"Then I'd never want to live down there," I said. "I'm melting."

"That's why they have siesta. I'm going to siesta all damn summer. I hate this. It's too hot to think."

She was 18 then, I was 12. I was trying to read a Nancy Drew mystery. Nancy was prowling through an old lighthouse in a cool, ocean breeze, but my arms were sticking to my armpits. There was only the faintest whiff of air from the slow "perpetual-motion" fan Dad had built once they started the energy conservation.

After more squirming and complaining about the heat and her boredom, Laura finally said, "Screw this. Let's go for a bike ride. At least we can get a breeze that way."

Poor Laura. All she wanted to do was go off to college, meet new boys, try out different versions of herself—all that had been promised to her. She was young and pretty, a little self-centered, smart enough to make something of herself when she was good and ready. Then our world was suddenly upended. With the economy so shaky, she hadn't found a summer job. On top of it, too often she had to hang out with me, the kid sister. Recently she'd decided she wanted to be called Lola. We never remembered, which gave her one more thing to be cranky about. After all, we were each clinging desperately to routine in our own ways, hoarding familiar names or habits—Dad tinkered, I buried myself in books. We were all cranky in our grief.

That day, Laura and I smeared zinc oxide on our faces and necks in bright streaks and put on sunglasses and brimmed hats. Laura's was straw and had a snug crown. Mine was too big, a hand-me-down of blue canvas, and

Mom had punched holes for a grosgrain ribbon that could tie under my chin. Laura smoothed sunscreen on her bare and shining legs, which always fascinated me. My one experiment in shaving the baby-down on mine had ended badly. We got our bikes out of the garage and I followed her down the alley.

The parkway ran 20 miles along the creek, down to the river. Its bike trail had been popular because it was normally green and shady, an island of cool in the city where herons stalked silently. But that May, the parks and yards were brown, the trees still wintry skeletons. Laura rode across the crosswalk at 42nd Avenue and turned left onto the trail, pedaling hard. The whole scene was eerie, the dormant landscape with the summery heat on my back and bare arms. There was an instinctual wrongness that sometimes made my stomach lurch, my pulse trot. Water splashed and glittered in the creekbed, still fresh with runoff from up north, I suppose. Stiff twigs poked my forearms or shins where the brush hadn't been trimmed—most of the parks employees had been furloughed. As we came around the big curve before the bridge, Laura suddenly stopped and leaned over her handlebars. I almost hit her.

"I can't stand it," she said. "Goddamn it!"

I scooted up alongside her.

"Look at that bunch of dumb, dry sticks there," she said.

"I think they're lilac bushes," I said.

"God, everything's ruined," she said, wiping at her eyes. "Everything's goddamn ruined. THEY spoiled it, with all their—crap and me-me-me generation and . . . .

Now people are worried about ozone holes, drought and famine, like we're some freaking African desert country. Mom and Dad still talk about college like, Oh, such fun! And Homecoming, yay! Like everything's normal—but I see the looks on their faces."

"Laura, they're only trying to help—"

"Lola, call me Lola, damn it."

"Shut up!" I said, "I don't see why you changed it, anyhow."

"Everything has changed, you just don't get it yet," she said. Her face was mean, pinched closed as she leaned over the handlebars. "There's nothing left for us! Mom and Dad, they knew they could do what they want, get married, buy a house, have kids, retire . . . a future. Don't you get it? That's gone, there IS no normal anymore." Then she threw her bike on the asphalt and bellowed at the sky—a howl, like an animal. I didn't know what to do. She was scaring me.

"Stop it," I said. "Just stop it!" I dropped my bike, grabbed her arm, but she jerked it away. She stomped around, yelling and waving, then she sat on the brown leaves and dead grass and started really crying. "Dammit," she gurgled. "Dammit, dammit."

Tears welled up in my eyes; I squeezed them shut, squeezed my knees together. The streets were quiet on a Saturday, what with gas rationing, so the crinkle of the stream was loud. By July, it would be a mere trickle along its unsheltered course. I hunched over my knees, sweating. "Please," I whispered to no one in particular, "please, please."

Laura's outburst stopped as suddenly as it had started. She got up and righted her bike, brushed dry leaves from her shorts. Her eyes were hot pink. "Those lilacs," she said flatly. "They should be blooming so thick you can't see green on top. That's where I had my first kiss, with Tommy Salazar."

"Tommy Salazar?" I asked. "Tommy?"

"Oh, shut up. I was just a kid—your age." She turned her hard gaze on me. "But I don't know if you can afford to experiment. We don't know what's going on, if there will ever be another spring."

"Don't say that!" I wailed. "Why are you being like this?"

"Mom and Dad might lie to you, but I won't," she said. She started pedaling, and I hopped on my bike and followed, as usual, but I stayed a good twenty yards behind her. My heart was racing from something other than exertion.

As that summer deepened, and fears along with it, I thought this must be like the Great Depression, the Civil War—the blanket of despair that weighed on us all, the strain of worry plain on faces. There was a forlorn Independence Day, when fireworks were banned and everyone fled to beaches, where at least lifeless sand was "normal." I went to Camp Wesaunee with my friend Irina, but the woods were ugly and bare; only the pines held onto a few scruffy needles, drab as steel wool. The mosquitoes were fierce, and we had lots of handicrafts and fencing indoors instead of woodlore and nature hikes. We couldn't even have s'mores—no bonfires allowed.

The President kept calling the catastrophe a "meteorologic anomaly," and soon everyone else did, too—some called it "the President's anomaly." They hadn't yet fixed on the sunspots or guessed how our atmospheric shield had faltered. There were theories and finger-pointing about auto emissions and coal plants, draining of deep aquifers for suburban sprawl, deforestation, damming, space debris. Scientists dickered with religious leaders who cried "Armageddon." Experts dithered and sputtered. All that seemed left to us was blame, a bitter sport we could do in place of mowing lawns and picking vegetables. It was a sorry replacement for hikes in green woods, splitting juicy watermelons. It was a sorry replacement for hope. In October, there were no leaves to "fall." Even our vocabularies were altered; we chose to measure time by months instead of seasons, chose conditional phrases. My sister was right—everything had changed.

One weekend, I came upon my mother crying in her small sewing room. She hadn't done much sewing since I was young, but it was the one room in the house that was hers alone, filled with her thoughts and belongings. She leaned on her work table, head in her hands, a soft drone of anguish rising and falling from deep within. When I touched her shoulder, she jolted.

"Oh—I'm sorry, Mom," I said, rubbing her shoulder. We were all learning how to give comfort. "Are you okay?"

On the surface in front of her were pages torn from a pad, filled with colored pencil sketches of flowers. Her seed catalogs and gardening books were stowed under the table. Some flowers, like tulips and daffodils, I could name, while others seemed fantastic inventions.

"Oh, I'm being silly," she said, running a finger below each eye. "I know they're only flowers, not important, like crops—but I miss them," she said, and two more tears dribbled down. "They have personalities, histories. After a while—they're like old friends, you know?" She tried to smile.

"Your drawings are nice, Mom," I said. "I didn't know you could draw like that." I picked up a page: strong strokes amid soft shadings done with the flat of the pencil, curved petals and stiff leaves. "What are these ones with the lily-pad leaves?"

"Nasturtiums. Do you remember, sometimes I put the flowers in the salad? They taste peppery." I could tell she was trying to put some strength back in her voice. She flipped the sheet. "Impatiens, I usually bed those under the lilacs. Pulmonaria, bleeding heart, wax begonia. Butterflyweed—that's good in poor soil." She shuffled through pages etched with color, now patiently explaining, an arm around my back. The names rolled from her lips; some sounded like diseases, others like beautiful women, like the names of neighbors, lovers, old friends: alstroemeria, ranunculus, black-eyed susan and veronica, liatris, perovskia, dahlia. Cranesbill, bloodroot. Shooting star. She seemed to draw strength from them, remembering. I picked up another sheet of drawings and she sighed. "Things I always wanted to plant but never tried." She patted my back in a way that showed she needed the gesture. I followed her gaze out the window to the dead, brown back yard. "I just don't want to forget," she whispered.

"Draw them all," I said. "We'll keep them."

Downstairs, Dad was reading the Sunday paper in the living room. The light had gone out of his face, as it had for all of us. He and Mom were often tired and worn-looking when they got home from work, and I was secretly glad when Laura would kick up a fuss with some petulant demand or angry outburst—anything to get some vitality flowing in the house. When they raised voices and Laura threw down her purse or slammed her bedroom door, railed against rules or an unfair universe, it showed we had some life in us yet. I was no help; when I was scared, I tended to hide.

Dad's face relaxed a little when he saw me come in. "Hi, punkin," he said.

"Hi, Dad," I said, fingering the arm of the sofa. "Would it be—Can I sit with you? For a little bit?"
He looked up at me and opened an arm, and I squeezed alongside him. I used to sit with him like that all the time when I was little, maybe with my blanky or a picture book, the two of us breathing rib to rib, silently. I was getting to be all legs and arms, but it soothed me to lean against him while he pecked a dry kiss on my forehead, and spread the paper before us like a sheltering tent.

It used to be that spring came in April. Tender grasses emerged; lawns and house gutters filled with soft, brown bud scales, shed hulls, while the trees' tiny leaves or blossoms emerged. My father would scold the mess on his windshield, muck the gutters below the maple with a gloved hand. Years later, with gnawings of envy and nostalgia, we've come to recognize the way we played favorites, our cult of summer. Sure, we'd given winter its due. There was the excitement of first snow, the unpacking of cross-country skis, mittens and sweaters in brave colors. We made the best of it—we northerners are nothing if not practical. We are realists, people of root cellars and engine-block heaters, of acceptance and making-do, gleaners and savers. But by March, we'd be sick of cold and our dreams of leisure were festooned around green yards and barbecue grills, cabins in shady woods. Summer was the crown jewel of the year: fat, rich months of sweet fruit and short sleeves, romance and ripeness. And it wasn't just the warmth, but especially the ripeness, the buzz of growth all around. For these green months we saved our weddings and graduations, family reunions and festivals. We celebrated our annual return to the bosom of the earth and the animal nature that we denied in fallow months with foundations and walls, our pelts and hides. Spring was the gateway to Eden, the return. Come May, we'd sink fingers into cool black loam with a sigh of relief. We'd admire the blooming and leafing trees and praise their shady limbs instead of huddling around their burning trunks. Come green, we came alive, emerged from hibernation, regained our limbs and loves.

So I see in hindsight. Our yearnings for this haven't changed.

Six years after that barren March, we've learned to hold tight rein on our hopes. Now, late February to early

March is when the buds announce our fate. Either they will swell and fill, or they will drop.

In the dead years, we reap only a harvest of tiny, dead buds. We have learned to rake and pocket even these sorry, deformed tidbits for some possible use: pickling, packing, mulch. Up and down the street, you will hear the scrape of garden rakes and shovels as we sob quietly over this sad yield, sifting dead hopes into tins and plastic bags, and return the tools to the garage after their only use. The budfalls announce that the mystery has done its work.

So our Februaries are anxious. Scientists holed up in National This-and-That Institutes have not yet found a tidy calculation to predict bad years, and the prediction would only extend the painful knowledge. We all have strategies for coping with the wait. My Dad's Februaries are wary of expectation. It's as if he dares himself to avoid looking outdoors for a sign, and he tinkers mechanically in his basement workshop. Mom hopes, with dreams of blossoms. But there is no help. A lack of sunspots alters the weather, or a burst of solar radiation shatters some coping structure in the leaf of willow or shoot of grass. We have tried waiting, planting a late June crop and hoping for a mild autumn of harvest. It does no good. People talk a lot about ingenuity and remediation in the years since it started, the "amazing" stop-gaps and storehouses and interventions to get us through. But that's not the point. The point is that our most basic assumptions have been sundered. My sister was right—nothing will ever be the same. Now I'm nineteen and it's my turn for college; we all want to be heroic scientists, to make a miracle. Still, I choose to think that, even in our stupidity, we were lucky—there was another spring. There continue to be growing years, just not every year. Spring is now a special occasion.

When we make it through March and buds unfurl, we weep with joy. We herd into the streets, crying and laughing. We break out the spirits we have saved, use up an extra week's ration of flour on celebratory cakes. It's manic and holy, rebirth and a Mardi Gras after months or years of Lenten abstinence. Farmers leave their make-do tchotchke-factory jobs and put diesel in their tractors, wait for allotments of seed. We sit on the porch and watch the branches sway above us, before us, try to see the leaves' gentle release, to hear the engines of photosynthesis. We thrill to the rare squirrels performing an acrobatic mating dance, a sight that used to be so common. There's a national holiday week for planting, and Lola comes home for a visit. She holds my hand as we sit on the front steps and sometimes my mother sings—we'll sit for hours like that, singing or silent, our eyes on the branches. All up and down the street, a hungry audience watches for shoots of hardy grass, the green twigs among the dieback. We give ourselves wholeheartedly to joy. We go to parks where we once played soccer or softball and help them plant oats and wheat, and we pray to all kinds of nature gods for gentle rains. We dust off ancient fertility rites; we dance, bow our heads, leave offerings. We've lost all shyness about thanksgiving.

Only my father is fearful of celebration, in his own pragmatic superstition. While we sing, laugh, he watches silently from the porch for a few minutes, then squeezes my mother's hand and goes to the basement, the house's perpetual dark winter. He cleans off the covers that will soon protect our barrels of rain from July evaporation. As I feel the gentle sun on my face, I know he's down there opening drawers and taking from them Ziploc bags of precious seeds—sunflower, melon, bean—and his tubers of Jerusalem artichoke, shrunken potato-eyes. He counts, measures, plans. Fingers gently trace the contours of hard pods, tough rhizomes. His hands give thanks for the blessing through a gentle touch of each hull. Perhaps, down there in the dark, he at last gives vent to a sob of gratitude and relief, presses his palms together, and allows himself to dust off a few carefully hoarded words: "sowing," "harvest," "spring."

A Short Treatise on the Effects of Genetics and Environment

Sonja sat on the bus, tightly clasping her groceries and her new worry: giantesses. It had hatched slowly, as worries go, revealing its elongated neck and knobby knees over the course of days. The world was off kilter, tilting strangely on its axis, teetering toward extremes. She had suddenly awakened to the facts, and she was worried.

They were everywhere, taking over; she could see them through the streaky bus windows. Tall, stretched-out women had always peopled billboards and magazines, but now there were more of them on the street, towering before her in a grocery checkout line. To Sonja, these gangly females were like plants fed fertilizer after weeks in a dark closet: they outstripped shape, went shooting straight up, forgetting to leaf. The men, too—towering high schoolers, pro basketball stars over seven feet tall. Donnie had figured out the trend, Sonja thought; he was hedging his bets. The bus was taking forever.

At an average sort of size 10, five-foot-five, perhaps average in intellect and ability, Sonja realized how easily she blended into the averaged build and beigeness on the bus—and therefore she didn't stand a chance. Her parents' durable genes had already decided her form, her place. She started to shiver, even though it was warming April. With the stresses of the past week, her body sometimes started shaking, and it would be minutes before she could will herself still.

Sonja reached her apartment a half-hour before Marcía was to arrive. Donnie had left another message on her machine and she erased it. *Hi, it's me—Sonja, are you there?—Pick up. Aw, pick up, will ya?—We need to talk*. She wasn't falling for that again. The day before, she'd given in and picked up, heard his jibber-jabber. "Be quiet," she'd barked, surprising herself. "Bequietbequiet. Shhh. Can't you see I'm off balance?" She'd hung up and sat on the floor and told herself, not yet—I'm just waiting for a sign, a landmark.

Now Sonja set the table and tried to banish her worry. She coiled clean cotton napkins into the silvery napkin-rings—one decorated with a sea horse, one with a sand dollar—soothing, oceany things. She pulled an onion from the fridge and peeled it, holding it arm's length away over the wastebasket. How could she have missed the obvious? In today's media-enslaved culture, it was all about having the proper form, appearance—forget substance. Obviously, Donnie wanted that ideal. A leggy ectomorph, wave of the future. Give it a couple of centuries, she thought, turning her head from the onion fumes; the tall getting taller, the small getting smaller, diverging into two sub-species. Sonja felt resoundingly average. Her hair averaged that drab color between blonde and brown; she had an average span of torso between bikini top and bottom, but it rode on the thick, powerful legs of a pit pony. They were not racehorse legs. She and Donnie were about the same height, but come to think of it, he was all trunk and short limbs; she was longer in the thigh-bones. Despite precautions, the onion made her eyes water. It was the onion.

The doorbell rang and when Sonja turned the knob, Marcía was halfway shrugged out of her coat-sleeve and mid-sentence, as if she'd been stored in the hallway since their last conversation. "—and the thing of it is, I left work fifteen minutes early and still, the damn traffic, it takes me forever to get here." She hung up her own coat, jingled and chimed into the kitchen, offered a green wine bottle, an enveloping hug. "I like that blouse, that's cute. So, how are you doing? Hey, you been crying, honey?"

"Onions," said Sonja, extricating herself. "I'm doing okay, considering. And work stuff, you know, they're changing our e-mail software and everybody's fussing, like it's my fault. Anyhow. Here." She pulled a waiter's corkscrew from a drawer.

"Right, e-mail." Marcía arched her brows.

They'd met in college, been roommates. Marcía, a big Puerto Rican woman, used to joke about being "imported color" at their largely white, Midwestern school. Her hands danced when she talked. She usually seemed on the verge of explosive action that never arrived; her presence always on low boil, the action imminent. Men were curious about that simmer, Sonja thought; they were drawn to some unseen metal in her, even though Marcía was not mantis-thin.

"Ooo, what beautiful tomatoes," Marcía said, watching Sonja unpack her grocery sack. "Like summer tomatoes, so fat. Where'd you find them?" she demanded, as if Sonja had stolen them from sunny dreams in their glass-paned nursery.

"They're hydroponic." She poured wine into blue-tinged glasses. "Salud."

"Ahh, they can't be as good as they look," Marcía said. "They look too perfect."

Sonja took another large gulp and began to wash the tomatoes. "Yeah, growing bigger and smaller," she said. "Giants and miniatures. More and more extremes."

"What are you talking about?" said Marcía, opening a tub of low-fat dill dip. "Hey, you got any of those baby carrots?"

"That's what I mean, baby carrots." Sonja said. "Baby endives. Toy poodles. And then, on the other hand,"—she weighed a softball-sized beefsteak in her average-sized palm—"two-pound tomatoes. Jumbo shrimp, for Christ's sake. People prize extremes. Soon there'll be no place for us average folks." She winced and began mincing a green pepper into shining cubes.

Marcía patted her on the shoulder. "Girl, are you sure you're okay? Do you want to talk about it?"

Sonja chopped fiercely.

"O-kay." Marcía eyed her for a moment. "So, when you want me to redo your apartment?"

"Soon."

"You were absolutely right to throw him out."

"Okay, you know I didn't throw him—" Sonja's hair suddenly veiled her face as she bent over the board, as the knife chop-chopped.

"You're too good for him! Too—Good—" she jabbed a finger at Sonja's face, at her half-hearted protest.

Sonja evaded the finger, slid the vegetables into a bowl and took the fish from the fridge. "Just a minute," she mumbled.

Donnie had cheated on Sonja. There hadn't been an adequate showdown, just Sonja crying and asking for her extra key back and Donnie sputtering explanations; but still, Sonja wasn't ready to say that Donnie had forfeited his place. Technically, she hadn't thrown him out since he didn't actually live there. Her equilibrium was off. She didn't even have the energy to be angry.

"The problem—" she finally told Marcía well into dinner and her third glass of wine. "The problem is . . ." her hand floated and dipped above the table, "is that Donnie and me go together. Salt and pepper, yin and yang, all that."

Marcía leaned forward and halted Sonja's hand with her own. "Problem is, Sonja, he's looking somewhere else. And I'm not saying that to be mean, fact is fact," she said gently. Her accent strengthened when she drank. "I mean, this isn't some *telenovela*, some soap, where he gets to play musical beds. He's broken, you can't trust in him no more."

She speared a piece of fish swiftly.

Sonja's eyes started to drip. "But he always—"

"Nah-ah-ah," Marcía warned, mouth full.

"Don't you even want to know—"

"Nah-uh!" She wagged a finger, chewed ferociously, swallowed. "No more Donnie, *el fin*. A man cheats on you once, he's spoiled, he'll cheat on you twice. I'm saying this for your own good."

Sonja and Donnie had been together eighteen months, enough that she felt accepted as herself. She was well aware that Donnie had faults, too: he had a little beer belly; his legs were too short, and sometimes he didn't listen carefully. But that's just wholeness, she thought, that's accepting the whole person, warts and all. She wasn't sure she could accept such a betrayal. "I miss him, you know?"

Marcía patted her friend's hand again. "You need some good luck. We'll get you fixed up when I come *feng shui* this place. Get the bad energy out of here."

Marcía had been on this *feng shui* kick for a while. Sonja knew only that it had something to do with different walls for money, love, health and so on. Marcía said that if only Sonja got the arrangement right, the proportions and angles of her environment in harmony, then the aspects of her life would line up as easily.

The familiar furnishings of Sonja's apartment seemed to sway slightly around her. "Oh heck, we could start tonight, I guess."

Marcía's laugh gusted, billowed. "Oh, no. I had way too much to drink. I'll be putting the bed on your money wall or something, and *dios!* Honey, you don't need that kind of trouble."

Alone, Sonja rinsed the last of the plates, clanked the stoneware into the dish drain. The hot running water made her want a bath. Her head, overwhelmed by wine—almost two bottles between the two of them—was still buzzing. Wobbling to the fridge with leftovers, she came face to face with a picture of herself and Donnie on its door—an image she'd seen so often, she'd been numb to it. She shook off the magnet and shoved the photo in a drawer. She wiped the table, wrung the dishcloth.

She wondered if Donnie had strayed toward or from. Deliberate cruelty? Criminal forgetfulness, possession by demons, what? What other reason? She gave him sex, affection, time; they both loved hiking and playing *Balderdash*. She gave him space; she gave him *her* space, a bureau drawer and the left side of her bed. Space in her heart. How could someone who had slept with her, brought her birthday presents, taken care of her when she'd had her impacted wisdom tooth out—how could he just *lapse* like that? Brainwashed, convinced by all the signs around him that some more alluring creature—long, towering, slender—was what he should want? She scrubbed the soaking broiler-pan fiercely. Every man, no matter how toothless and awful, can picture himself with a pin-up, she thought. Or had he strayed instead *from*? From Sonja's strong, earthbound legs, her tender heart, her mostly pragmatic head that stayed level and well below the clouds. Clearly Sonja, in her averageness, was not suited for love, destined only for competency, for maintaining budgets and unjamming copiers. For the past week since her ugly discovery, she felt merely dull and reliable, a prototypical worker ant. She kicked at the bottom cupboard.

She hadn't decided whether she wanted him back. Now, he was like a piece of furniture coveted in a store window that suddenly looks less appealing when you get it home. She poured out the last inch of wine, rinsed the bottle.

Maybe it wasn't his cruelty or her personal failings but something larger—like sweeping evolutionary forces. A trend shaped by global warming, a shift of entire populations—toward taller and thinner. Nature had nothing against Sonja—there was no need for anger. Just worry. If I were a tomato, she thought, sliding one into the crisper, they'd just slip a gene in somewhere and in two generations I'd be new and improved, statuesque. Hell, if giants are the wave of the future, I need to be with a taller man, anyway, her tipsy logic continued. Our kids will be above-average height and their kids will breed giants, round meaty progeny. Bigger, more resistant to spoilage. She tied up the trash bag in a neat bow.

Then the shaking started again, quivering through her torso, down her elbows. She held the sob locked within her body and there it shuddered. From the fridge, she took out a jar of minced ginger. Then a carton of orange juice, an ancient container of wheat germ; nutmeg, olive oil and honey from the cupboard. She wedged the containers carefully against her chest, where her tremor made them clink together, and juggled them into the bathroom. She ran water in the tub and twisted the plug, poured and scooped her condiments into the bath. She peeled off her layers and unsnapped elastics, carefully stepped into the water freckled with clots of wheat germ and ginger. It was too hot and she breathed staccato and tried not to cry. "Softens your hands while you do dishes," she mumbled. "I'm soaking in it."

It had been two weeks and Donnie was still calling. Sonja let the machine screen calls. They were always the same phrases in varied order. *Sonja, are you there?—it's me—We need to talk.—Pick up.* The digital recorder distorted his voice so that it sounded like he was underwater, slow and bloated. As far as she was concerned, he had capsized the dang boat and thrown them both in the drink; let him find some heron-girl to wade out on her long legs and drag him to shore.

Sonja found reasons to work late, meet friends for coffee, so she wouldn't have to navigate the silent tracts of her apartment. She took more baths, pumiced her elbows and heels. She knew she needed to dust and do laundry, go through the mail, scrub the tub—take charge. The last of her remaining greenery, a spider-plant, needed some TLC. It was sending out long runners which sprouted perfect clones in a last gasp of survival—or maybe just an asexual attempt to repopulate the window. She did none of these things. Instead, she made lists: *get new plants, be more perky, learn a new language, read at least a little Tolstoy, try yoga.*

Still, a rough day at work always set her mind spinning. There were no other answers forthcoming, from Donnie's plaintive phone messages or Sonja's wilted spirit. At the bus stop in the cold shadow of the Federal Reserve Bank, all it took was a tall, bony, horsey-faced woman stalking along the other side of the street to spur her obsessing on the new world order. The tall of all colors would triumph, while the compact and sturdy, like Sonja, picked green beans and crept into offices to clean. Sonja, imperfectly proportioned, an office manager with a flair for organization, would be left behind. So what if I'm *nice*, or *loyal*, or a natural blonde, she fretted; the stolid genes of Sonja and Marcía would become extinct together as the twiggy giants took over. Even Marcía, who was in law school––even the indomitable Marcía would be left behind, due solely to her five-foot-nine, size-16 frame, though it was well shaped, though it had boldly sported the costume of Xena, Warrior Princess at Halloween. Only the dark tresses and brown, glinting eyes would be left of women like her, the way red pea blossoms win out over white. Sonja's own pallor and recessive-gene skill of tongue-curling and who knew what other gifts would be lost in the process. Had something gone wrong? The world should belong to vibrant, big-hipped women like Marcía, she thought; women who loved life with a toothy hunger, the kind of women who laughed loudly, who cried at commercials and yelled at feckless taxi drivers and pounded the wall or their lovers' shoulders with their fists when they made love. Women who were more than just sturdy. The kind of woman she'd rather be.

Marcía came over with supplies: notebook, compass, an octagonal chart and a paperback titled *Find Happiness Through*

Feng Shui. She circled the living room like a shark, expectant. The early spring sun was warm through the south window. "We're gonna get you fixed right up, honey," she said. "We're gonna clean up those energy suck-holes and bad angles and get some good fortune swimming around this place. You got any iced tea?"

Sonja wasn't sure how rearranging furniture would change her luck, but if Marcía's system could help her get her bearings, she'd give it a try.

She delivered the tea and tapped a women's magazine on the coffee table. "The tall ones self-select, you know," Sonja said. "Remember my friend Betsy? She goes to this Beanpole Club so she can meet men as tall as she is. We're toast."

Marcía gave her a funny look. "The beanpoles can do what they want. Me, I go dancing so I can meet a man who knows how to move his hips, treat a girl with some manners. Got to have both," she winked. "And quit changing the subject."

At Sonja's scowl, Marcía laughed from belly deep and wrapped her in a big hug. "Aw, I know you're hurting, honey." She was trying to stifle her laugh, and failing. "*Mira*, those scrawny models—don't you see them with little short men in the tabloids? Little rich Arab men, little balding Italian CEOs, little Argentine soccer stars. No, it will average out to little, round, brown babies. I'm gonna be in the majority any day now." She wiped an over-flowing eye. "Nature knows about balance. And in ten years there'll be some kinda dark Albanian beauty, some Latina big-ass girls on all those magazine covers."

"Okay, but they'll be tall, skinny Latinas," Sonja said glumly.

Marcía rummaged in her patent leather tote and pulled out a pen, a compass and some other papers. "I know why you're talking this crazy talk, and we're gonna fix you right up. It's not supermodels, it's not you, its your surroundings. It's all about balance." She walked through the apartment, measuring, scribbling, and Sonja followed. Marcía was sketching a floor plan. She circled through this space that was supposed to complement, define, and shape Sonja. She played with her octagonal chart. "When were you born, again?"

Marcía consulted her book, jotted. She sat next to Sonja and showed her the floor plan, her home reduced to a grid of lines and boxes. "Okay, you got some bad angles in here. You gotta move your bed over here, for starters," Marcía said. "The problem's there, just like I thought. Your marriage and relationship sector is a mess. Your prosperity sector could use some help, too. And this part over toward the kitchen, we call it the 'disaster' area, but that's not really what it means, exactly."

Sonja slumped back into the hand-me-down sofa. "My kitchen is a disaster and my love sector is a mess. I knew that."

"Look, missy, you want me to help you out or not? You don't even have to believe in it. If you can't take charge of your love life, you can at least get a handle on your apartment."

"Just get on with it, already." Sonja waved her hand limply.

Marcía pursed her lips: *stubborn child*, the look said. "Okay? It's about balance and energy flow. It's dark over here; that's bad. You need to put in some little mirrors, maybe some crystals, a lamp to attract some light. Clean up the clutter around your closet. You should get some plants in here."

"I like plants," said Sonja. "I used to have a green thumb."

Marcía spoke and pointed—a pinch here, and dart there, like she was fitting a dress. "You're ruled by the element of water. That means you're sensitive, intuitive, and easily influenced, but I don't need a book to know that, do I? Your colors are blue and black. You could use metal in some places, since metal feeds water-people. Over there, get yourself a little picture of some ocean scene."

"And that will help my love life? A trip to Pier 1 Imports?"

Marcía threw down the pad, threw up her manicured hands. "Hey, you wanted me to do this, don't make fun a me. Remember how my back was bothering me so many months? I was sleeping under a beam that went right over that part. I moved my bed, the pain was gone in a week. I put some little mirrors in my prosperity area, and I won fifty dollars on a scratch ticket. It's all about freeing up pathways for energy, *chi*—the life-force. Balancing the yin and yang, you know. Letting your natural strengths shine out. What's it going to hurt, huh?"

"Sorry," said Sonja. She leaned forward. "I appreciate it, I do. Tell me what to do to make it work."

"You don't make it work, you let it work. Just be yourself."

"If you say so. How'd you learn all this stuff?"

"Old Puerto Rican tradition." Marcía looked up from her sketch, laughed at Sonja's expression. "Oh, come on. I took a class at the public library."

Sonja said, "I don't think Donnie cheated on me because the corner is dark."

"Honey, I know. Does it really matter why? Is there any explanation that would do? No. And men, they've got some funny ideas about us—good girls, bad girls, dumb-blonde jokes, and they always look at me funny when I say I like classic rock—as if salsa's the only thing for a *puertoriqueña*." Marcía shook her head. "Look, I'm writing it all down for you, all right? It'll make you feel like a fresh start." Marcía handed Sonja some pages from the notebook, the book, floor plan. "I have to admit, though, I did like that Ricky Martin. He's hot."

Sonja threw herself into the new obsession. She exiled *Glamour* and *Self* under her bed and read the book that Marcía left for her. The whole point was to keep life-energy circulating. It all seemed to revolve around lines and angles, corners and oppositions, light and darkness. Mirrors deflected bad angles, filled in missing pieces, but leaky faucets sapped energy. She bought some crystal prisms and mirrors and put them where her friend had suggested, shifted sofa and end table, ordered throw rugs from a catalog. She pushed Donnie's side of the bed against the wall. But that wasn't all; energy wasn't confined to space and objects, the book said. It was the life-force of the body, too. The "chi" came in through the breath, the pores, as well. Restored energy would release her hidden talents and graces, her good fortune.

Sonja practiced sitting tall and "breathing in harmony with her space," but it brought no great revelations; she still found herself making lists of self-improvement projects (*bake bread, be assertive, learn to tango*) instead of "watching" her breath. When her thoughts strayed to obsessing, she'd have to jerk her mind back to the bellows of her lungs, and picture warm exhalations as aqua-colored mist. For some reason, it was aqua. All in all, that was a bit more comforting than feeling like a genetic dead-end.

One Saturday, as she curled in the tattered armchair freshly draped with a bedspread, she admired her new plants, a ficus tree and a broad-leaved dracaena. But she didn't like the placement of a round planter filled with bamboo where Marcía had suggested. What the heck, she thought, I'm supposed to be intuitive; she picked it up and moved it nearer the window. The sun shone through the leaves and dappled the floor.

Sonja couldn't tell if the life-force Marcía talked about was moving any more freely, but she liked the notion that she was somehow encouraging her luck, her destiny. Donnie had called three times that week but she was still letting the answering machine pick up. She wondered if screening calls was bad *feng shui*, if the unanswered voices would somehow pile up and dead-end, their energy strangled—although Marcía said that anything using electricity kept currents flowing. Once she had felt like picking up the phone—like screaming at him—and the sudden energy of anger shocked her.

When the doorbell rang, Sonja assumed it was the UPS man and was surprised to see Donnie, elongated and top-heavy through the peephole. She left the chain on, and let the door reveal a slice of his form.

"Hi . . . Sonja." He paused as if he'd started to say "honey" or "sweetie," and changed his mind. "Um, can I come in?"

"I don't think so." She felt tears pushing behind her eyes. It felt bad to be standing with the door between them. "What do you want?"

"I've been trying to call you . . . I think we should talk. I made a mistake, I've said I'm sorry, God knows I'm sorry—" He kept talking and Sonja was trying to reorient that stripe of him, of reddish face, *sorry*, one eye, short calf. To keep from crying she tried to fix and register each displaced feature; then, tried changing them—a new nose, a thin brow, would that help? Would that change things? He was saying, "to realize, babe, and I'm just asking for a chance, that's all."

"Give me a minute," she said. Light reflected onto the side of his face, his ear, in shards slanted by the mirror. All this time she'd wanted to ask him why, WHY? But would she feel any better, could she forgive him, if he said he was enticed by some gazelle-woman, if he was just bored? How could she ever know what was fixable? "Just one minute," she mumbled, pressing her hands over her forehead.

"Okay. Take your time. Yup." Donnie's visible eye stared past her into the silver-framed mirror. "Hey, is that new?"

"I'm a water person. I benefit from the presence of water, the color blue, metal," she prattled, shifting on the balls of her feet to hide the shaking that had started. "Geez."

"Huh? You haven't, like, gotten into Scientology or something, have you?" He laughed nervously.

"Shh," Sonja said. She was wondering if the mirror could reflect Donnie right back out of her life, and if she wanted that. She looked at the piece of him in the doorway, broke him down into sectors, angles. The good parts, the good parts. She stepped behind the shelter of the door.

"Donnie," she said, "I need some time to think."

"Well, if you need more time, that's fine, but . . . keep an open mind. Hey!" he yelped, as she pushed the door shut, latched it. His voice was slightly muffled now. "Are you okay? You sure you haven't joined the Moonies or something?"

"No," she said. "I'm not a Moonie, and I'm not a freak." Her voice rose. "I'm—a sensitive person, Donnie. I'm a good person, I'm caring, and maybe you should have thought of that. Now, *go away*."

"Sonja, honey, I know . . . Sonja!"

On the other side of the door, Donnie muttered, "Aw, gimme a fucking break." She slid against the foyer wall and waited silently to hear his footsteps shuffle away. She squeezed her back and legs against the cool plaster to try to quell the shakes. Take charge, take charge. You could rearrange things but there was no guarantee it'd improve, that any of them knew what they were doing, she thought. Sonja looked up and saw herself in the mirror, quaking.

What wall did that represent, that little expanse? Longevity, knowledge, disaster? Maybe Marcía's plans meant you could only change your outlook toward the future, your sense of direction. There were things you couldn't change. The past. Donnie's red face and short calves and his excuses. Sonja's strong limbs and the way she was shaking. Maybe she'd filed certain feelings in the wrong places, where their energies were blocked. She tried to breathe deeply, to let stillness wash through her.

Sonja caught her profile in the mirror again. Giving up the wall's support, she approached her reflection, strange and familiar. She noticed the geometry of her face within the silver frame; how its square made sense of the human shapes and angles, the way the metal made her eyes stand out, color of winter water. All the variables: wood, fire, metal, water, earth, breath, compass points, external rules and influences, giantesses on the loose, bad habits and bad karma—too much to account for, she thought. There was no knowing. You could only try to see yourself clearly and make adjustments. That was the trick: which frame.

She shuffled over to the armchair and sank into it. A little sob burbled up, almost escaping—and it felt okay. Maybe the shudder was easing. Maybe it was okay to stop trying so hard. The pot of bamboo, the sinuous ficus, stood calmly before her in the window's light. Sonja thought, they didn't tremble, didn't worry or compare themselves to their neighbors. Each was complete—concerned only with the energies from without and within, sun and water, the spiraling pulse within the seed that makes it burst its hull, an intent to grow.

THE SUN SAILS BROAD REACH

I found him in a yellowing book from a library whose patrons seemed as old and used as the volumes on the shelves. A tight-lipped summary, an index to old notarial records: my distant ancestor had contracted for two years to be a *voyageur* in the interior of New France—today, Québec. A traveler, an explorer; another who shed home and family to go searching. I had to go back centuries to find him, beyond the amnesia of immigrants' offspring; my past is the silence of northern snows. What little I know of my family, bookended solidly within the 20th century, shows a penchant for staying put—at least until the migratory jet age, and I belong to that, a generation that sees the American continents from the sky, the way their mountains crumple and peak like bed-sheets; that feels a mandate to move because we can.

First I'd gone east, and we were all adventurers, young and moving for the sake of movement, all dance and gesture; like fish, we needed motion just to breathe. We schooled in downscale music clubs and coffee shops, on tumbledown porches, worked a shifting grid of loves and friendships. Failure and heartache hold no magnetic pull; that's the nonsense of novelists, and our hardships were what happened on the way to work, the grocery store, not destiny. After a time my friends found pairing paths or welcoming soil and settled; they shelved me, stored my telephone number in a book, a shoebox on the shelf. They'd bring me down every two (or three or six) months, conjure my presence with the telephone's bleating. Then back I'd go to their memory-closets while they returned to mysteries of diapering or mortgages, new romances demanding concentration, other adventures they didn't want to share, that turned them inward, burrowing.

Eventually, I shed that Atlantic-coast city like a grimy, brick-colored skin, and went looking for my perspective again, westward—the direction of surveyors and voyageurs. In my new rented space, everything still hovers in cardboard boxes, except the astonishing amount I left behind—curbside, Goodwill, in cupboards of others—even loves and friendships.

And the man who made me move was that distant ancestor of mine, my kin spirit, wanderer. I find him, and his story spurs me to action. His claims: a journey, a homestead lacking title-deed from the Abenaki or Huron peoples, the temporary title of explorer. A Northerner, I know his black winter dormancy of pine and hemlock amid the white hush of snow, the green humming summers, the tea-colored rivers. The "new" continent is the only world he knows, as natural to him as it was strange to his French peasant parents. During those wandering years, I wonder what he sees from the high-sided bark canoe; how he views native peoples or missionaries; if he fears unknown beasts or rapids to which the river might bear him. The thrust of rivers is his only compass. Perhaps it matters that he goes forth and comes back—does not stay in the bush and become a trader or trapper, following the mink, beaver, and fox, does not take a Mohawk or Huron wife. He returns to his birthplace in the fledgling colony, puts down roots, a respectably planted *habitant.* There he lies, forgotten by the Minnesota-transplant line, until I excavate him from frail pages. I find hints of that life—christenings, burials, ownership—in grainy microfilm. His time as a voyageur is recorded only as a few dates, a few *sous* in wages. I wonder how he chooses his home soil. How do his travels mark him, what calls him home?

Like that forbear, born in 1670 in the cliff-walk town of Québec, I have a limited contract, explorations to be made on the way to somewhere else. I've come back to the plains. Almost home—the region I'd been born to, where the horizon resists change and chasing. I have come to find words to say what I mean, to see meaning, to say what I see and where it might be going—to chase a dream of beautiful science. Expanse is plain here. Beneath the damp breath of Erie and Huron and their *portages* and *traverses*, on this ancient flood-plain, nothing halts the sunset; its colored fringes wrap around even to the east like an embrace.

For years, I'd felt hemmed in, by escarpments of geography and of months, coastal limitations. For some reason I failed to notice how my roots eluded soil, the failure to thrive; I stayed and took a drubbing. I imagine a quivering, myopic glaze to my eyes. I sloshed through centrifugal whirlings of a calcified, class-bound coastal city, an inescapable circling of event, let myself be carried along. There my instincts seemed to hibernate even as the land was overmastered: clay and puddingstone paved over, rivers dammed and culverted. All referents were of humancraft. I bobbed in an eddy of career (or was it *job*)—the accepted mode of self-definition. I witnessed weddings and sat the death watch. I swirled through the social square dance that often left me with an ill-suited, rhythm-deaf partner, or none at all, while the ones I wanted swung by, arm in arm, carried past me by insistent music and a caller who saw me only as a square in the orderly quilt of the dance. Eddying: motion, but no progress. A secret charm I never learned to sing. Maybe I never got the tune right, or the tide-tables. I lost my bearings, with no cardinals, sun a goldfish in a narrow bowl whose sides were hidden.

Now I've uprooted for a temporary stop where there are horizons and soil, a whole ecosystem to absorb. Place is a workshop and I will be planed, punched, honed in unfathomed ways. The people I call family will never see this place—for them it stays a brief change in an address-book, mythic as a hidden north ripe with silky pelts. This patch of prairie has become a way-station for the selfish luxury of learning, a left-hand turn from my elliptical trajectory. *But your career*, people said, *but you were settled*. And here I am, in a university town in the cornfields, geared to intake and output. Endless harvest of green freshmen to struggle with sleep in over-warmed classrooms, practice puking their under-age beer. Each batch is complacent fodder for this year's mononucleosis and Greek rush, malleable minds almost willing, almost awake enough, to be nourished. In this cycle, four years later and the grad students are still sweatered and grumpy, seniors cocky and sporting rings with dates engraved, or bearing diamonds, or rings beneath their eyes; an acetate-robed parade, product available for delivery. Nobody stays long, by design, except the few who dig in like walnut trees, settlers, to oversee the rented life, the small-town youth and semesterly comings and goings with the sameness of songbird migrations.

The town derives its name from another way-station, a transitory past-time. It evokes town squares in France where the old men gather beneath the *platanes*, pale-shouldered plane trees whose limbs are pruned back to knobbed, arthritic stumps. At small plots and parks the men gather to smoke dark cigarettes, drink *pastis*, and play *pétanque*, scooting the varnished black and white balls along the grass. They wear flat, dark caps and talk about the weather or the football match or local politics. An alternate existence might find me at the pitch where they assemble to sort things out, share opinions, gain perspective. A stop-over between noonday dinner and the work that strains the shoulders, stains the fingers that chuck the *boules* back and forth; a through-station, not a destination.

There's relief in long vistas; I can feel the earth breathe again. Here a great ocean floor once upthrust to land. Land settled into a great dark swamp excluding man, land was invaded and reshaped as plains acreage, man-drained of muck, of bladderwort and moss, of mosquitoey vapor.

Here at the university of land oversea, things change yet retain some wholeness; I take a lesson. The text lies here in plain sight if you only know where to look, if you follow the gurgle of hidden water, check beneath the canopy for the berries, hear the silence of hiding that signals a hawk high overhead. It's all here, soaring overhead; underfoot, in the lime-laced topsoil. I want to lie in it, the crispy, prickly greens and yellows, the thin-leaved plantains that sprout from lawns, goldenrods with their sneezy offerings, purple asters, brittle Queen Anne's lace and bitter milkweed. If you lie down, let the growth poke and scrape and ooze through you, let the ants and grasshoppers click, yellow-jackets buzz. Allow the voices to speak. All just minding its own business of roots and stalks, fleeting photosynthesis, sunflowers' faces following the sun. All the buzz and tickle seems to say: If you recalibrate circadian rhythms, let yourself feel magnetic north, listen to the blood song, perhaps your animal instincts, dead from domesticity, will begin to awake.

Forgive thc circles, they are nature's way: the droplet ripple, a hawk's elliptical trajectory, curving here to there to here again, past to present. I circle back and find the voyageur; he sends me packing. If I gaze at the horizon long enough, maybe it will come to me—not the horizon but the sense of it, the edge, the boundary where knowledge ends or begins. Maybe I can look back toward that hill-girt coast, where the horizon was a nearlooming bowl, and finally see where I've been—a place so dense and crowded with person and incident that they cram together like bodies in a subway car where everyone bumps but no one really touches. Crowded, but without touch. Does any of that matter now? If I've been annealed, does the memory of the fire bear mention?

The magic of synthesis takes such care, and I left the city feeling a mere catalyst, nonreactive. In an entire large, elbow-bumping city, all the weeks spent on pursuits I enjoyed and those I thought, medicinally, would be good for me—all the praiseworthy or dull desk-hours, all the parties and first-dates—I still left there with only the faint half-life of touch upon my body, a stale memory of intimacy. *Intimité* means the same, in French, but *intime* also means hidden, secret. Intimacy hiding beneath the sludge of dailiness, waiting. The explorer seeks a river's *intime* source, fertile swampy bottom, rich salt-marsh, matted green. I carry a sense of direction in my flesh, a needle aimed true, not pulled by metals. In my forays into the wilds of love, I was not always the one who turned back. Yet how can anyone complete the journey without a map, ill-provisioned as city people often are, so secure in their recognition of near landmarks and buzzwords, the look, smell, of class or race or occupation, false scents? Where appearance is valued over import. Not so on the plains, where you have to seek out the hidden aspect, value beauty of function, trust a whispering token in the blood, think about survival.

I don't expect much here—it is a limited engagement. We have work to do. We are here to open our eyes, to discover something. It is supposed to be off balance. In the lab, all is orderly. Expression of intent doesn't guarantee desired results, but there are formulae, and paths laid down before. DNA has its own language, and the syntax of nucleotides must be followed for the genes to do their work. Outside the lab, there are other rules. Uses of the verb "to want" have their own taboos. I want a cup of coffee. I want this assay to yield a clear pattern. *I want* other things, but they are deep and instinctual, couched in terms of fate, intention. A statement of desires won't help me find them; it must be coupled with question, search. Then there are social conventions and feelings to consider; egos, old failures, new apprehensions, and I wonder how, in our dense cities, our cliffside colonies and prairie outposts, we can stay so separate in our journeys, and how it can ever work between two people, how it is that I've ever made friends, chosen a lover, or let myself be chosen.

Alone in a crowd like a point mutation, and as common.

Outside the lab, inside my body, under the broadloomed sky, I'm not even sure how to frame the question. I have no hypothesis, no strategy. Skin, the largest organ, goes neglected and the second-largest, brain, is over-taxed. Skin, buffed and soaked, oiled and softened, goes hungry. Skins mere bundles on the quay, awaiting Atlantic voyage, awaiting transformation into furry luxuries. My self of skin and muscle, of lust and hope, is lost while my brain lolls around the lab and posits explanations. The "social animal" clusters in crowds but seems afraid of touch and gesture. Yet even the cat knows to seek a warm leg to curl against. Domestication means choosing another as "home." Peer review among fellow females results in exasperated sighs; huntresses scour self-help books for clues. We clink beer glasses, assert we don't want to become *those* pathetic women—*those*—the undefined other, outcast, savage. The women of my past are mute about their heroics, their journeys barely mentioned. The voyageur's mother was marriage-fodder, shipped to a strange continent with a dowry from the crown; a great-grandmother sailed from Germany, alone in steerage, age fourteen. We need no dowries, nor husbands. But we stumble when we see those less savvy in woodlore, surely less hardy and heroic, inhabiting that satiated space. Surely it isn't so impossible for us. We think we want traveling companions in the wilderness or the safety of a stockaded village, but we're not sure; desire, even abstract, is so stubborn. We fear equally to give up the trail. We have no answers and weak hypotheses. For now, we have a respite: We are here to work. To shiver in the bark canoes, struggle through the portages. Our contract bears no care for cold feet, isolation—our task is to make it back with tales to tell.

Our minds captain us now, mapping and surveying, recording the geography with ends in view; compilers of evidence, mercenary, calculating. The heart simply follows the water, searching only for where it leads, hanging on through the rapids, floating or straining, watching, a compass of sorts, certain of nothing until it is revealed: the hidden headwaters, the great lake, the continental divide, the legendary sea.

If I can only take what I know and what I sense—spread it out over acres and acres of green and gold space, items on blankets at a yard sale—maybe I can begin to find a pattern, choose directions. The dispersion of my family of birth, the accretion of faces that passes for another family . . . all the leavings and leave-takings . . . love-takings . . . migrations . . . a predator curled in a basket, its fangs faintly showing. If I rearrange the colored blocks, there's a new quilt, Log Cabin or Flying Geese, a different orientation, the foreground and background reverse. *Settler or traveler?* If I rearrange the words, the actions, will love come of indifference, wisdom of loss—will leaves curl and flutter down, reveal the moccasin-trodden trail we've traveled? Will the shift make a new compass?

The sun inscribes a circle, the circle is the image of oneness, and it is the oneness that one desires. All our atoms of time and space keep changing combinations. We call our geologic epochs *school*, *work*, *marriage*, or call them *me*, *you*, *us*, or otherwise unbalance our natures with false dichotomies and sequences. We work and miss love, love and forget art, create and neglect faith. When do we have time to look up from the absorption of the discipline, the intoxication of love, the glory of atoms and bonds and reactions, and calculate the weight of our other parts? Calculate positions from the stars? Yet somehow we choose the ground that is home.

The French come to the plains in borrowed canoes. They establish toe-holds with terror and trade. First comes Cartier, naming the rise above Stadacona "Mont Royal," halting his sailing ship when rapids block his way to China, switching to bark boats. Later explorers follow the rivers—La Salle, Marquette, and Père Henepin, whose exaggerated chatter of a cataract, a mere sixteen-foot drop, draws others toward the upper Mississippi. They butcher native syntax and leave their names behind, littering the Great Lakes', the Great Swamp's fringes with French. Samuel, Sieur de la Champlain, veteran voyager on return visit to the thundering St. Lawrence, ventures from Cartier's outpost in summer 1613—a foray with four men, two canoes. They struggle with so many portages around the daunting rapids, vicious June mosquitoes hardly smudged away by evening campfires, the downed pines to work the carried canoes over, under. Champlain, arms laden with arquebuses, paddles, cloak and whatnot—small wonder he dropped the round brass astrolabe, the one engraved "1603" for his first voyage west. Its loss, the uncharted latitudes, go unremarked in his accounts. There it lies for 250 years, moss-draped, reckoning no declinations, cornering no stars, until that primitive, hardy stuff peels back its green nap, and there a boy sees a glint, a golden wheel. The circle circles back and finds its way to Montreal, the forests it once traveled now shorn.

Perhaps my wandering man, my ancestor, traced the same river down, west; perhaps he went north, up the river named for the Huron, or the one named for Cartier. He's left me no maps, no stories, only the round coins of his wages recorded in an upright hand, some token in the blood for survival of long winters. A craving for rivers, broad skies and starlit nights so I can fix my place.

And I've come back to the broad expanses to catch my breath, recalibrate, where there is still soil, a growing season. Here in the open, maybe I can find my bearings. Here you can see the sun move, the Great Wheel; say what you see, see what you mean. Reflect on distance. The relief of a far vanishing point after claustrophobia of narrow-shouldered hills, bricked in by mud of human history. The bliss of space, the immense distance between one person and another clearly apparent. I know the fear of the unknown and of being known. The plains give the necessity, the joy, of discovery, of blazing a trail through the sea of grasses and having it swallowed up behind. Strange voyageur, the heart, running those turbulent waterways toward an uncertain end, still formulating its questions, its measures. Trying to stay afloat. Homing toward the level-headed flatlands where impossibilities embrace and an embrace is impossible. Where a predator, deprived of instincts for its own kind, sheathes claws, curls happily against the belly of its preoccupied mistress.

Behind me are scraps of legends. Seven brides for seven brothers, Acadian strand of my past, those immigrant *poitevins* who tamed the marshes. A legend of the buried fork: A milk fork wrongly used for meat must be buried in the ground beneath a full moon to make it kosher again. My uncle swears he tossed the cat over the garage roof fifty years ago; my grandmother insisted he couldn't *possibly*: fact or fiction? The legend that the baby must be baptized quickly lest it die unconsecrated. In old Québec a child is always named for the godparent—an uncle, a best friend—the church registers form a map of kinship, a braid of names. I have been told so little of the past; my grandmother says *Gezundheit* when I sneeze, and a great-uncle pens memoirs of Rhode Island textile mills. In the absence of stories, the old words—*kosher*, *Gezundheit*, *habitant*—form a portable descendance. But not a map. All I have are scraps.

If I were buried under the whispering grasses for a month, would I be made whole?

I came of age and traveled because I could—east, the route to history. I spun in the tidal vortex. I searched, queried those tiny photographed black-and-white faces that once inhabited a green and rural Brooklyn, mill-cottages of Bissell's Cove, the plains of southern Québec, all their footprints halting at the fretful Atlantic. If I lost my compass in the drink, I dredged up a missing past. My forbears traveled light, obsessed with forward motion, jettisoned private pasts. In with the Europeans, I find a Micmac woman's blood is mine; it travels in bodies of the fleeing Acadians, and the loss of her name, her words, her names for what she didn't call the New Brunswick coast—the loss of all their names and tongues and ways stacks up bone-white, talc-shale and limestone, tiny lines in tomes of dry, decaying paper. I've been given no songs, no lineage. It's as if my grandparents tried to hatch themselves, parentless, so squeezed and pressured were their pasts, their stories and languages, by the white hands of fears, mores and misapprehensions.

Stories exhumed: lives entwined with a ribbon-factory in Chemnitz, and a jacquard-tape mill in Rhode Island recently turned condo. When the Great War begins, my great-grandmother in Brooklyn stops speaking German. A great-grandfather in the thirteenth state sings sweetly to his wife in French when he dozes after dinner.

Stories held dear and silent: Waiting through the war to come of age, my father never gets his heart's wish, to helm an airplane like his brothers. His hopes are grounded by his blood pressure, a trait that had just killed his mother. In his telling, though, the devastation was transferred to another story of that spring—he had to quit the baseball team to help his father at the store. The truth comes after his death, from an old and tiny, ballroom-dancing aunt.

The pulse of longing remains shrouded, grown-over. I'm given only decorous scraps of history to shore me up, gray slate shims for a mortarless Rhode Island rock wall, pieces of a lost art. One generation or ten, the untold routes they would have taken, a vast unpeopled silence, ice-locked and snowbound.

Snows are sparse here in these drained plains and in summer, among the familiar, other strange trees introduce themselves: sweet-gum, with its starfish leaves and fruit like anti-ship mines; lobed-leaved tulip trees; and scab-barked sycamores, bone and brown, like the old riverside specimens back east, like the French *platanes*. Here, it's the smooth calm bottom of an old ocean. Things creep the floor or soar above, swooping and diving like skates. It's similar to home, same skies, yet not. I was born in sight of the Mississippi, its quick brown slide between steep limestone shelves, calciferous bones of old seafloors stacked and shingled.

True to my migratory century, I wonder what the turn of a calendar, or catalpa, leaf can mean for my destination. I am torn between wants: to run rivers and sink roots.

I've yet to find my own true tree-shape to hide in, perched along some lusty riverbank. I collect the sight of birds and bugs, count my days, wonder where the boxes next will stack, near what water table, salt or fresh, near what indigenous fruit and stalks. *Shhh*, they say. *Shhh*, those figures in homespun on the childbed, at the frozen water-bucket, with the clam-shell tools, along clever dams that tame saltmarsh into wheat fields. *Shhh*, let it be; what do they matter now, our longings? What does it matter now, if we were voyageurs or conscripts, adventurers or refugees? Take a lesson: Creep close to the trees and disappear. Love the grasses and forget their names; continue.

What did my ancestor find in his travels? Did he go seeking an imagined destination or thinking merely of his return? Did he have visions, or was he absorbed in demands of his belly, his cold toes, sunburned skin? What stories were allowed space in that narrow vessel? How did he convey, in Micmac or Oneida syntax, *I want*?

All it takes is one hawk—a slim harrier, a broad-tailed buteo—to soar and see what living goes on below. A falcon nabs a songbird, in a shrill dive from a half-mile up. The hawk masters life and death as long as it carves the air high, with a broad view of contours below, of shape-breaching motion of life—too close to earth, it is blind-sided by near dangers. It is useless on the ground, loping awkwardly toward fresh kill that even a tiny weasel can defend. Swinging silently overhead, the bird of prey sees the embracing circle.

Back on the plains again, the sun sails broad-reach and

I smell north. *Habitant ou voyageur*—settler or traveler? I appeared well situated but was spinning down a funnel. For now, I serve the cool ministry of science; but beyond the lab, I must learn to see again, rename things, before I can discover. I must know a swampy island in a sea of grasses. I wait like Circe, the falcon, watching the horizon, trying to remember the words to my song of forgetting.

I will move on, in search of the ground or life that feels like home, unsure what sign will inform me. A good black loam, a quality of light, some hard and hardy vegetation? A silent signal inside? I am trying to weave the current skein and the broken threads of my past into a plain and useful blanket; learning to pack lightly for the trip. More questions and answers lurk down the edge of that endless horizon, among patches of silhouetted trees. I just can't see them yet, or name them. The hawk, all eyes and instinct, dark shape soaring, sees me better than I see her. What is it our hearts see so clearly, chase so restlessly? What does it take, how many miles, before we can see the course of our own lives? Before we finally see the destination, darting like a mouse below the swift-falling shadow.

All This Talking About God

The brightness that sustains me is meant to blow away. Almost every day, I walk down to the college to watch the Buddhist nuns. The young Tibetans fold themselves crossed-legged on the wooden platform, funneling colored sand grain by grain onto a chalked pattern in the center. They wear cloth masks so their breath doesn't scatter the sand. Grain by grain, color by color, creating a circular mandala, the house of a god. It's the only thing that brings me peace, makes me forget my empty hands. Silently they pray as they work. Four at a time they bend over the great wheel, heads bowed, hands curled, shaping, as patient as stalking cats. I guess they believe life is only suffering, but they seem so contented.

Talking to God, that's all some people talk about, at the bus stop, laundromat, the bank. They are full of advice, stories of the Lord's personal favors. I know that the black woman is supposed to thump on her Bible, serve up the family dinner, and call on God to help her keep it all together. I know that's my place. But since when did I ever do what I'm supposed to do? Still, these people keep at me, talking about their gods. Even on TV, the running back in the end-zone says, "I thank God, he was with us today," because his god is a Jets fan, his god does not listen to the pleas of the Miami quarterback, the Denver coach. I am told many things by many people anxious to help. They claim to talk to God, and he (or she) tells them things to tell me, things to make me change my ways, my whys, things to make me see the light, to open my heart, and so it does; the chambers open, open, shut, shut, like hands in prayer.

How I'm raised to judge myself: Woman is the pillar that holds the roof when other support gives way. She is the anchor, the rock, guardian of her family's health, spiritual and mental. So where does that leave me? I couldn't help my baby. I'm no help to my husband. I haven't been on speaking terms with God for years, and certainly not since Daisy died, and her so little, not even talking. People keep telling me God has a plan. If that's so I'd have to believe He had something to do with her death, too busy taking calls from football players and soap-opera actresses. Who can suffer a God like that? Even cruel nature seems more kind.

She was such a little thing, eight months, and her symptoms seemed so slight. When I called the doctor back and said, she's still fevered, they weren't really worried. We took her to the hospital, then everything went horribly wrong. The fever kept going up and there lay my poor baby, packed in ice like that with all the I.V.s. She was blotchy and puffy, and then she just quit on me. Something went, her liver or kidneys, then her heart. The doctors leaped in, blowing air into her with a bag, shocking her chest. Even they were shaken. A matter of hours. I could say I prayed good and hard but frankly, I didn't have time to mumble one under my breath. And I could say that bitter trial strengthened my faith, but it wasn't much to begin with, and after—well, just another thing dusted over by neglect.

Then all this crazy comfort, talking about God. Some fool gives me a coffee mug with the story about the one set of footprints in the sand and why, God, did you leave me in my heartache, and God says, that is when I carried you—a coffee mug, as if that will mend my heart, clear my head. Well, carry me or not, we aren't speaking now. Somehow it never took root in me. The church of my childhood was custom more than devotion in my household. My mama, as intelligent a woman as you'll ever meet, a teacher, wasn't particularly devout, and she's got her reasons. My grandma used to "get the spirit" and it seemed to me then, a girl in pigtails, like a demonic possession. Not the Word, a bird, fluttering epileptically inside her. I only saw it happen once or twice; she rarely came to visit. She lived down south, and my mama had a strange pride in saying she would never set foot in Alabama again. We all have lines we won't cross.

Gerald and I work at the phone company. Gerald is a lineman, out in all kinds of weather, up in the cherry-picker, rotating night shifts. It was always Gerald I worried about, not Daisy. Out in ice storms with the downed electric lines and all. Daisy was safe and warm at home with me. She would grow up, have her chicken pox and skinned knees, get her grown-up teeth, have birthday parties, learn her times tables and be someone. It was my husband in the dark storm I worried over.

When I went back to work, they all knew about Daisy, so I didn't have to excuse my bone-tired stare. Checks kept coming in and I kept them credited right. Credits and debits, cool, clean numbers, safe enough; people pay a lot to talk. Lately friends point out to me it's free to talk to God. That big hearing ear, big piggy-backer, enfolding hand; he's all there in bits and pieces for some game-show winner, but who's minding the store for the rest of us? Charlanne just sat quiet with me at coffee break, for which I was grateful, sometimes rattling her braceletty arm toward me and putting a warm hand on mine. Just keeping me company in my devastation. No chatter about taking up the burden, following in His footsteps. You don't talk that trash to a grieving mother. You don't go around saying that her baby girl is in a better place.

One day on our lunch hour, Charlanne said, "Get your coat, we're going out." We walked down the street to the college. In a room with high ceilings, almost like a chapel, the Buddhist nuns worked quietly. They sat on a big platform in their maroon robes; their heads, shorn to black stubble, all looked alike as they bent over their work. Charlanne and I pulled up chairs and watched the mandala take shape. Now I go back almost every day.

They are Tibetans living in exile in Nepal, here for some special occasion at the college. At moments when they take a break, smiling, chatting, we realize that they are just girls, college-age themselves. One of the older nuns, perhaps my age, takes me by the hand. Her English is good; she has a lazy eye. Smiling, she explains their rituals, the symbols of the mandala. It represents the home of a deity of compassion, with a central medallion, the four gates, a symbolic tapestry of color. In tempera-bright colors—red, yellow, blue, dark and pale green, orange and white—they sift tiny lines: scrolls for clouds, religious symbols, small rain-spouts for the palace roof. The patterns are bright and fine as embroidery, a quilting of sand, held together by nothing, yet whole. She nods toward the altar, explains the offerings of flowers, waxy cakes, incense. How they asked the Dalai Lama (I guess that is like asking God) to be allowed to learn the sacred art from their brother monks. For this act of devotion they'll gain merit in the next life, my guide explains. They'll dismantle the mandala in a ritual, to return the blessings to the earth.

Sometimes the nuns climb down and refold themselves before the altar at the far end of the room, each clasping a bell and a charm of bronze like interlocking figure-eights. I don't understand what they're saying, but they're talking to God with fine, curling, undulating hands, low chanting that rises and falls. Then they shake out their limbs, chat for a bit, crawl back on the platform and pick up their narrow silver funnels, their meditations.

The pattern must be a mystery my heart knows, not my head. I come back as often as I can.

"These things just happen sometimes," the doctor had said, meaning to be kind, laying a hand on my shoulder—a young woman like me, tired and stunned. "The infection was just too persistent. I'm so sorry."

"Don't tell me that, sometimes—not to my baby," I'd cried out, throwing off her touch. "Don't gimme no *sometimes*, there's my girl, there's supposed to be antibiotics, there's supposed to be—" One minute in my arms, the next, small and lifeless on the bed. I collapsed against Gerald, his own hot tears washing his face, knowing I should be comforting him, that he needed me to hold him up. But I had no strength. We cried into one another's neck and shoulders, our baby girl before us with a tube in her arm and the mask off her face, done with struggle; cried there without pride, without hope, as the hospital shuttled all around us.

She was named Danielle after Gerald's mother, a tall woman with a long face, soft-spoken and fiercely dignified. But I called her my little Daisy. She was born February 7, eight pounds, twelve ounces, with a little mole above her butt on the left. She was only eight months, still at the breast, a child with a sunny disposition, a curious expression of surprise on her fat cheeks, a squeaky laugh.

I took a week's vacation and lay around the house crying, or stone-faced, unable to. My mama came for a few days, quietly took over the kitchen, let me cry when I could. "I should've taken her to the doctor sooner." Cold, like it was someone else's life, a movie I'd seen. "Tell me what to do, Mama."

"Times like this it's hard to find your way, I know," she said, rubbing my back.

Gerald and I passed like ghosts, not saying much,

brushing closely past each other, grazing fingertips, curling desperately together in bed for fear the other would vanish. I made myself cook him proper dinners, meat and vegetables, potatoes or biscuits, so he could keep his strength up. I couldn't eat. My breasts were still swollen. I had to express the milk with that pump, everything flowing out of me, all milk and tears, leaving me empty. The doctor said I'd have to stop soon, to let my body adjust to the absence of suckling. Sat in the rocking chair with my hands empty except for that damn breast pump and my body grieved for my child, my arms aching for the weight of that little warm shape. It took all the will in my slack body to do the dishes at night, to rake myself out of bed before noon. Sometimes Gerald got the coffee on, washed the pots.

One morning, passing the half-open door to the bathroom: Gerald's face is lathered up but only half shaven, his palms braced on the sink, his head hangs, he's crying so quietly I hear only breath. I hushed past. He used to curl her on one arm like a sack of flour, a football, tickle her chin with a finger to get that squeaky duck laugh. For some reason we tried to smile bravely at each other, but it was grotesque and we sank into wordless touches. I felt like I had no voice.

It's Gerald I come home to, but I don't like being in the house alone. I make excuses to go out, invent errands; the botanical gardens, the mandala-makers, movies, window-shopping. One day I'm driving to work and I hear an ad on the radio for the zoo. I think of toucans and flamingos all day as I sit at my keyboard. It's not far and I stop on the way home, pay my three-dollar donation. I look at the birds but they don't hold my interest long; the gorilla is throwing his poop at the spectators. My feet take me to the cats.

When I was little I begged for a cat like my friend Donetta had, but my mama had a horror of them, I don't know why—some ancestral voodoo nonsense. I walk down the ramp into that cat smell, and I can see the pens are too small, though they've tried to shape them with landscaping and all. A Siberian tiger sleeps on a concrete ledge, its back pressed against the thick glass, half an inch from my hand. I could tap on the window and I bet the big cat wouldn't even jump. The sign says there are new cubs, but I don't see them. Her fur looks stiff as wire, luscious black and white paintings on her face; the bristly whiskers twitch occasionally, a paw as big as my face flexes. Some hunting dream.

In the next pen the leopard is restless—pacing, pacing, a lopsided arc around the oak with its clawed bark. The sunken enclosure must be a good half-acre, but he is hemmed in, no horizons; the autumn sun gives little heat. He belongs someplace huge, the African savannah scorched yellow, not in a grimy northern city. Tongue lolling out, he stops, pants listlessly. I know this look, this dulled perseverance. The look says, what are we doing so far from home? Where's my sun? However did we get here? Capture, displacement.

On my way out I pass seals barking, begging children for fish, a polar bear swimming laps in the too-small pool. Someday we would have taken Daisy to feed the seals. The smell of fish makes me want to cry. I am late to make dinner.

Gerald knew when he married me that I didn't claim faith. Man and wife four years, and I still marvel at his. My husband, he's got a man's God and a man's minister, all sanctifying and testifying, scouts all in uniform, merit badges shining. I love Gerald—but his words have no more wings on them than mine. Yet he stands up and sings his hymns, accepting grace as his due. I sing, too. Oh, What A Savior. Someone's singin', Lord, kumbaya. Go tell it on the mountain. Someone's singin', Lord, but it's for my own comfort; preachers know the power of giving voice.

Gerald is a kind man, quiet like his mother, confident, without anger. He goes to his church and comes back full of rescue. The world owes him better for his uncomplaining patience. I owe him better. I should be his rock, but right now all I've got is blood and milk, tears and sweat, animal things washing through me, things that don't bear reckoning. I'll suffer through and give him what I can—my love for him is primitive and holy. He's my sun. I can't help it; I love that man more than I could love any god.

I know it's a jealous God in the Old Testament, envious of a woman's love, her ability to bring forth life. Woman is fierce in her loving, like a cat who owns you, commands you or is your equal. A cat wants to sleep up against your heat, to breathe in your face, share your space as close as possible; then walk away, walk the perimeter on the fence-tops before she comes back. A cat has secrets. A cat could talk to God. Never a dog; a dog only wants to please master, whatever the cost. All these people throwing platitudes at me: "Offer it up." They only understand a god they can be subservient to, give up their will to, cast off the burden of their own hearts and minds. "Give over the burden." They want me to hurry up already, get it over with, a sudden resolution—as if grieving has a deadline, like it's not a long, hard walk.

In bed I listen to Gerald's breathing go loose and soft; his hand brushes my hip. As I start to doze I see the leopard looking for its big sun. The tiger twitches her paw, her whiskers. Why can't God be a creature like that? A sensual creature, a thing with fangs and claws. An instinctual god, no promises, no preaching. My spirit has longings, too. I need a god that wants us to dance. One two three, one two three, a fine old waltz, scandalous. A holy roller shaking in the ring of a great colorful circus. None of us want to feel so small, so alone, shut off from the sky. But I need power here at hand: old gods out of the forest, all kinds of howling juju and Mary in her motherly sorrow, animal spirits. Beside me the tiger stirs and growls. I feel her warm back pressed against me as in some deep dream she prowls her territory, sniffs the Siberian air, recalls only in sleep the scent of freedom, some other way of being.

The nuns are serene as ever and I can tell the mandala will be finished soon—the huge wheel is almost filled with intricate shapes, a colorful fever-dream. My guide, the nun with the smile and lazy eye, says there remains only the lotus-petal border of white sand. Her name is Domo. The blessings multiply as they work and pray. In a few days, she says, it will be completed, then demolished, because the devotion of making is enough; nothing is permanent.

Domo says the gift remains precious, not less cherished for being destroyed. I guess their gods, too, have ways that come to us as mysteries. In the end they will sweep all the colors together, carry the sands in a procession to the river, return the blessings to water, to earth. Maybe someone will be talking to God meantime, among the waving tangerine sleeves and shaved heads, cymbals and horns. Yes, I think, that's right. Shouldn't we dance behind the nurses, the hearses, to celebrate the freed soul, give back its many brilliant reds and oranges and blues to the dark water, stars in the pond? But no; we mutter, wear drab, drape in crepe. Did so, myself. Did not raise a mighty noise. Back into the brown earth, brown child.

It's a Saturday, just three weeks after we lost her, when I send Gerald out to the store. I've been wearing a cabbage leaf in each bra cup because the doctor said it would help stop the milk flow—folk wisdom, not medicine. But after a couple of days, the soft crinkle and cabbagey smell is making me so sad, I go to the kitchen, peel the wilted greens from my breasts, throw them in the trash can. I take out a box of old friends—Mahalia Jackson, the Clark Sisters, Cissy Houston—music, what's left of my faith. I pull out an old record of the Terrell Sisters and I turn it way up and let the gospel music full of praise and sorrow wail up around the walls, splatter over the furniture, slide along the floors. *Guide us through the storm, oh Lord, through the bitter rain,* they sing. I go into the little room we'd made into Daisy's nursery with the flowered curtains and wallpaper border. *My Lord, oh my Lord, speak to me.* I know these songs not just by heart, but in my heart, harmony and melody; hymns, that's what I've kept from church-going.

I go in there with boxes and I take out the clean clothes, the onesies and the tiny T-shirts. The little pink knit sweater and cap, the frilly dress from her Granny Danielle, ridiculous for a child so small. *Is there only darkness? Only pain and strife?* I sing along. I take those things and the tiny booties out of the little drawer and I fold them neatly and pack them away. The little ribbon bows for the barely kinky hair she barely had. The shoes. The plastic pants, little towels, all the while my eyes burning with tears. *Do my prayers fail in darkness?* Stand on a chair and take down the mobile over the crib, tear off the light blankets, put them in a bag. I start to choke on the words while I let my madness out, singing hard. I pound the wall with my palm, I shout out with the Terrell Sisters, *No, no! The Lord shines down a light*—but it's just howling. It's release but not rescue, just more tears clacketing through my back, my ribs, the wailing that has to come. I take the sheets and the toys *Do my tears go unheard?* and stuff them in a bag to burn them, burn them all, all the traces of the infection that robbed me of my baby girl. Scalding, hacking with sobs, resolute. I turn the record over and get a bucket of hot suds and that's where Gerald finds me, on my knees, scrubbing Lysol over the crib, walls and everything and wailing at the top of my lungs because Deena Terrell can sing *Awake to Miracles* but there wasn't one coming for me.

"Don't do this, baby, don't do this," he says, taking the brush out of my hand and wrapping his arms around me. I can see he is scared, of me, of my passion; he doesn't see it's just the body's alarm. I hold my hands out to the sides with my wet rubber gloves and howl some more, till I can get a grip on myself. "It's okay," I say between gasps. "It's okay. I'm okay. I—just been quiet as a church-mouse, so quiet, and I need to cry, I need to yell. Oh no," as the tears well up again. My body has the rhythm of the sobs and it won't let go. "I just need to cry for a week of Sundays." Tears in his own eyes, he lets me go, pats my back and nods, and I stand stupidly crying in the middle of that room with my yellow gloves dripping, and wave my husband out the door.

I cry, I sing, I yell till I'm drained, then I put out the boxes of Daisy's things. I ask Gerald to burn the small bag of sheets, the few crib toys, all infected, tainted—to burn them, burn, I want to see my rage done up in kerosene. He shakes his head at me, no; no, girl, goes and pushes the bag deep into the trash can.

So the sun keeps rising and somehow Gerald and I do, too, something to be continued, and hold our breaths or silences, and hold each other. The future seems heavy as a roof. And so goes all this talking to God: those Black Muslims down the block calling on Him a dozen times each Friday, the Jews who don't say His name, and earnest Christians, the football stars and the bottle-blond rappers testifying. But I need a God more fierce and close. Maybe it's me, in my loss, in my need, that can't cotton to theology, sermonizing. An old-school African nature-god might suit; some long, masked face that speaks in dance and movement, music instead of testaments. She needs to come shameless and simmering around my leg, saying, You're mine. A god who wants my speech, she's got to take it. She's got to say, you and me, we're attached; then maybe I'll start talking. She's got to make me hers, rake her claws up and down my shabby bark, mark me with her fine, scented whiskers, and yowl.

More than ever, it's hard to find my place, my breasts still leaking unclaimed milk, my body missing my baby in ways that won't meet words. What's a body to do but go on—it's in our blood to continue. I guess maybe Gerald and I will have another child someday—I owe him that, too. But right now my body's still slack from childbearing and weary with grief. I will need to make up some kind of faith before then, a cat faith or a dog faith, something to hang my mortal hat on. I need something to cling to, otherwise there is just the sand sifting in a random dance. Things don't happen for a reason, not things like that—unless you give them a pattern to fit into, "God's will." How else does a people bear strife and loss, oppression and cruelty and downright evil? They say, "God's will."

I've got those longings for a thing that might be faith, a wheel swirling with color, a mystery only the soul and body understand. One day I may find myself in veils and trousers, like Khalila who found Islam and a husband in Cleveland. I might yet find my way back to Jesus. Maybe I'll go Buddhist like Tina Turner, like the nuns, and then I can learn to just *be* in the universe and lose my prideful pain.

If there's nothing else, there are the seasons that govern all creatures, music that dances in our veins, senses beyond knowing. Or I'll have to find some other way, between the parked cars and rainstorms and monthly bills, the blizzards in my heart, cyclones churning history around our ears until we fall down wailing—because that's what animals do, in the heat and the storm, without reasons, without shelter; we cry out, we endure, and we suffer.